MADCAP MASQUERADE

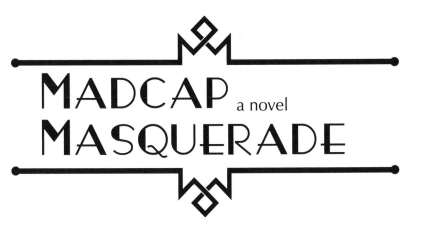

MADCAP a novel MASQUERADE

JANET CHAPMAN

University of New Mexico Press ❖ Albuquerque

Library of Congress Cataloging-in-Publication Data
Names: Chapman, Janet, author.
Title: Madcap Masquerade : A Novel / Janet Chapman.
Description: First edition. | Albuquerque : University of New Mexico
    Press, [2017]
Identifiers: LCCN 2017004010 (print) | LCCN 2017010836 (ebook) |
    ISBN 9780826358691 (softcover : acid-free paper) |
    ISBN 9780826358707 (E-book)
Classification: LCC PS3603.H372 M33 2017 (print) |
    LCC PS3603.H372 (ebook) | DDC 813/.6—dc23
LC record available at https://lccn.loc.gov/2017004010

Cover illustration: silhouette courtesy of Freepik
Designed by Felicia Cedillos
Composed in Optima LT Std 10.25/14.25

To my dearest Jessica, who loves stories

Contents

ONE   1

TWO   18

THREE   33

FOUR   48

FIVE   59

SIX   69

SEVEN   93

EIGHT   99

NINE   113

TEN   124

ELEVEN   145

TWELVE   152

EPILOGUE   163

Acknowledgments   165

About the Historical Characters   167

ONE

Amanda tugged on what was left of her hair and watched the floral curtains billow and collapse against the screen. Each time, they made a little thump and then a pool of dappled sunlight splashed along the sill. Moist air slipping around the curtains smelled like sunflowers and pine needles. In the street below, newsboys barked early-morning headlines from the *Daily New Mexican*. Something about President Coolidge. Germany and the League of Nations. An update on Rudy Valentino's cross-country funeral train. Fully awake now, Amanda pulled the spread up under her chin and surveyed the space, which she had been too tired last night to contemplate. Her immediate surroundings interested her much more than national news. Besides the bed, the room held a small pine bureau, carved in the Spanish style, and a worn, handsome oak dressing table. A tin sconce, embossed with decorative pin-sized holes and holding a candle thick with caked wax, hung on the wall. Her leather travel bag was tucked between the bureau and the bed, a heap of clothes was slung along the bed rail, and a dark-brown mustache lay precariously at the edge of the dressing table.

Oh Lord, what had she done? One less snip of the hair,

and she would have been eagerly chatting about Fiesta with June and June's mother over breakfast, a tableau that struck her as gloriously safe. Instead she found herself in La Fonda. What had she and June been thinking? Though she guessed June would be struggling with her own second thoughts right about now. Likely buttering her toast, eyes cast down, and wondering whether to tell her mother all. Don't, Amanda warned, screwing up her face and trying to send the message telepathically across town. She had taken on this—probably misguided—adventure partly to find herself. But this much she knew already. After making a decision, she always found a way to reconcile herself with it, no matter how crazy.

Not that she had much choice. This time, she pulled at her hair with both hands. Shorn grass.

Still, with Fiesta starting tomorrow, she was lucky to find herself in any bed, especially one in La Fonda. When she and June had concocted this scheme, Amanda's first thought had been of the landmark hotel. Since Fred Harvey had taken it over a year ago, it had become the center of Santa Fe's social life. She hadn't even considered there might not be any rooms. She owed this one to the good luck of standing, dazed, at the desk last night just as a telegram arrived with a last-minute cancellation. Probably best to accept that as an omen and get on with it.

She peered over the covers and studied the mound of clothing at the end of the bed, mentally folding each item and arranging them into a neat pile. It wasn't like her to leave things in a heap. Grey trousers, green plaid suspenders, grey shirt, white club collar, navy blazer, and serge driving cap, all courtesy of June's brother, away at law school. And underneath, a rose-colored sateen step-in. She smiled. Amanda's tall, thin frame and small breasts—who knew she'd be grateful for them one day?—were going to make it easy to disguise her body as a boy's. But could she manage to behave like one?

She had acted, she reminded herself—three performances as Rosalind in Wellesley's spring production of *As You Like It*. For a moment, Amanda basked in the sound of applause thundering in the auditorium. They had been convinced. Her spirits lifted. I can do this, she told herself. I can pull it off. She considered the males in her life, thinking how best to mimic them. Perhaps she could sit and stare at a newspaper, pages open to the financial section, like her father. Or, if she had to talk, converse endlessly about aeroplanes, like June's younger brother.

Or run off with the heir to a gangster's fortune.

The telegram had arrived in June, on her wedding day, alongside her eggs, sunny-side up.

Bachelor party speakeasy. Vinny the Claw's daughter. Married at midnight. Please forgive.

Signed, Elton. The man with whom she was to have exchanged vows in eight hours' time. She had stuffed the telegram beneath her plate and stabbed at her eggs like a pick into his heart. No wedding? No guests? No fifty years ahead as Mrs. Elton Smythe, gently directed in all things, high and low, by Mr. Elton Smythe?

A narrow escape, she said to herself now, though no one had dragged her into saying yes. She'd been delighted to be first in her class at Wellesley to be engaged. Despite being a 1920s New Woman—that's how she thought of herself, anyway—she had still admired the girls who were engaged by nineteen, married by twenty. Her engagement had placed her at the center of everyone's envy.

And Elton had been maybe not earth-shakingly romantic, but a very pleasant means to an end. A happily-ever-after end, or so she had thought. He had a great smile and a knack for compliments. If he had talked about himself too much—and he did, most of the time—she had learned to cover her face with an alert expression, allowing plenty of time to daydream behind the mask. Whenever the truth had begun to niggle—years of this?—she and Elton would somehow find themselves in his roadster, necking. Even now, the thought of those kisses made her a little woozy. Her body slipped under the covers, her shoulders snuggling into the starched pillowcase.

Stop it, she said to herself. She pulled herself upright.

No, the telegram had unleashed plenty of havoc but, surprisingly, precious little heartache. She was still distressed by the shame of the thing (left at the altar!), though at the time what had disturbed her most was the anticipation of a summer fouled by endless explanations. Really, Elton and Vinny the Claw's daughter? Had she missed something during those daydreams? Yet she could be proud of herself. Her solution—cajoling her parents into holding the reception anyway, minus Elton and the minister—had caused as big a stir among Boston society as Elton's defection. That evening, she had presented herself in the garden—among decorated lanterns, flowing champagne, and spirals of jazz notes—as Woman Scorned, draped in black satin and pearls. Amanda made sure, by revelry's end, that she had torn through everyone's curiosity like a reaper to wheat.

But the following day, waking past noon, her muscles

had ached as if every peck on the cheek had been a blow to the head. Gasping at the sunshine streaming onto her face like Hollywood lights, she had cringed at her identity-starved future. Her gallant effort had used up all available energy, and she found herself unable to concoct a new plan. Everything she recognized about herself had been tossed into the waste bin along with the telegram. She knew what a girl was supposed to do in her position. She knew what her mother's friends would say. But damned if she would *ever* again look for a husband.

So she had turned her back on love. Over two long, hot, soggy months in her family's home in Brookline, she had rejected all invitations and instead had holed up in the house, perusing newspapers, magazines, and books, looking for direction. Midsummer, Amanda had found a signpost. She stumbled on an entreaty from Mabel Dodge Luhan tucked into a column of titillating gossip about husband number four. From her frontier paradise, the article read, Mabel Dodge Luhan, New York's most famous salon-niste, was calling great souls to the American Southwest, a site of social and psychic renewal.

Great soul? Amanda didn't think so. But she was certainly in need of psychic renewal. And though she didn't plan to literally knock on Mabel's door, Amanda was at least familiar with New Mexico. Her family, a pillar of proper Boston society, had moved to Santa Fe for her father's health in the mid-1900s, returning east in 1911 when Amanda was about five. Amanda's best friend, June Sheehan, lived in Santa Fe still. So when her parents made plans to tour England in late summer, Amanda had begged them to let her visit the Sheehan family instead.

By then, she had armed herself with research on Mabel

as if it were a class assignment. Mabel was about her parents' age and also an heiress. Married at twenty-one, Mabel had seemed bound for a conventional upper-class existence in stolid Buffalo. But—and this seemed like a sign—widowhood at twenty-three had kicked Mabel in a new direction. In Italy, Mabel had presided over an expatriate community devoted to life for the sake of art. A decade later, in Greenwich Village, she had attracted the best, brightest, and most radical bohemians through her weekly salon. Now Taos, New Mexico, was the site of her self-expression. Along the way, she had taken on a series of husbands and lovers—her current spouse, Tony, was from Taos Pueblo—but Amanda managed to skip over Mabel's romantic preoccupations, concentrating only on her search for the genuine.

Since then, Mabel had become the lens through which Amanda viewed life. "Give the whole of yourself to what is ahead of you; to what you want to bring to light," Mabel had counseled in one of her articles. "Nothing dispels criticism like success!" Amanda discovered a banquet of appetizing precepts aimed at self-knowledge. Whenever one resonated, Amanda added it to her philosophical plate, now heavy with lifesaving morsels. "Of course, there are always some people who are afraid," Mabel had declared. "These people are to be understood, and pitied." Amanda pursued every form of advice. She wrote down her dreams. She opened herself to energy sources. She pitied those who didn't share her insights. She seemed always at the edge of revelation.

In Santa Fe, however, Amanda was forced to listen to those who were blind to Mabel's magic. Like June's mother, Mrs. Sheehan, who had actually met Mabel. The daughter of Mrs. Sheehan's friends, the Hendersons, had married

John, Mabel's son. The thirdhand connection thrilled Amanda. But Mrs. Sheehan didn't share her houseguest's raptures over the famous saloniste's philosophy, drily noting that her most prominent characteristic seemed to be self-absorption, not self-knowledge. She could behave generously, she admitted, but more often, Mabel was petty and domineering, a description that simply stunned Amanda. And she had found it impossible to credit her next words, aimed at "any of you New Women." According to Mrs. Sheehan, Mabel Dodge Luhan believed women should take a back seat to men. Their role, it seemed, was to serve as a muse to a man's creative impulse. On this subject, Amanda knew Mrs. Sheehan had to be wrong. Mabel was plenty creative. Amanda had just read a short story of hers in the *Dial* about Silverbird, an Indian from a northern pueblo, who had helped neighbors prepare for their daughter's wedding. The bride's mean-spirited mother sent Silverbird away before the feast, so later that evening, arm in arm, Silverbird and two friends danced and chanted all the way back to the wedding party, where they found the guests slumped on the floor as the result of their songs. After helping themselves to the feast, the three young men arranged the guests into pairs of enemies. "The sun will wake them," Silverbird said as they left. "I have told him to do it. Now we go and leave them to be cross with each other, not with Silverbird."

A tale of enchantment and Mabel's own. So Amanda chose to ignore Mrs. Sheehan's comments, which, though perhaps well intentioned, were clearly incorrect. To keep from annoying Mrs. Sheehan, Amanda did manage to stop inserting Mabel's name into every conversation, but she was unable to quit exclaiming about the joy of self-discovery.

The quest consumed her. The anonymity of her visit—only the Sheehans knew of the wedding fiasco—and New Mexico's shatteringly immense landscape, all sky and wide vistas, had provided ideal conditions for her pursuit.

The curtains snapped like gunshot, a gust of wind sending the mustache sailing.

Amanda considered the hairy little thing, floating, dipping, finally landing on the hardwood planks at the edge of the rug. Now, it seemed, she would add disguise to her complement of self-knowledge tactics. Besides helping June with Justin, this masquerade would give Amanda complete anonymity. Why, she couldn't even fall back upon her own name or sex, she had pronounced last night to June. Without anything of her past to hold on to, forced to depend only on her wits, it was the perfect opportunity to discover her core.

Starting now. She stretched her arms high, then swung her feet to the floor. She'd better get her core self moving, or nothing would get discovered.

By eight thirty, Amanda had ventured out of the hotel and was walking along Shelby Street, which bordered the east side of the Plaza. She stopped before the large plate glass windows of the Thunderbird Shop, the First National Bank, and the White House—a general store—straining to catch a glimpse of herself in their reflections. Every image gave her confidence—even she saw a young man when she looked—but as soon as she stepped away from one window she'd worry until the next view steadied her mind. At five feet nine, Amanda was as tall or taller than many of the boys she knew. Twenty years old, she had the physique of a stick, like one of the petroglyphs June had pointed to at the museum, with arms stuck out at ninety degrees, hands dangling. That was Amanda's opinion, anyway. Too thin, too tall, too flat. Though she used to have full, wavy, chestnut-colored hair, she reminded herself, complemented by high cheekbones and eyes like blue diamonds, or so her mother said. Attractive but not so feminine she couldn't pull off this disguise, she decided, trying to reassure herself on both counts. Parted in the middle, the new hairstyle made her look a bit like that dreamy actor, Douglas Fairbanks, especially with the mustache. Spirit gum secured that wisp of hair above her lip, but she poked at it every few seconds anyway. Her core self, apparently, was prone to tics.

She ran out of plate glass at Palace Avenue. The Museum of New Mexico took up the entire north side of the Plaza, housed in an ancient, one-story adobe building with windows that not only were paned but shaded by a covered walkway—the *portal*. Beautiful, but not what she needed. So she cut across the Plaza, a large grassy area with walkways and towering cottonwood trees. The Plaza functioned like any town square, including hosting the obligatory war memorial. But many of the businesses around it didn't look anything like those back east. The museum was just one of a number of adobe buildings that interrupted a line of two-story Victorian facades. The Victorian style had arrived with the railroad and infiltrated the town. But thanks to a group of passionate Santa Feans, some facades were being exchanged for adobe, gradually returning the Plaza to its centuries-old appearance, a look Amanda also favored. Her eyes lit on La Fonda. She'd never seen a hotel like it. The inn was several stories high, made in the adobe style, with sculpted walls enclosing a series of rooftop terraces. The brilliance of the sunlight drew out every detail of its earth-colored walls, as well as its beams, or vigas, which stuck out along each layered roofline. Even the shadows seemed part of the design. The sight made her smile. Then it was back to plate glass and reflections, this time in front of Zook's, a popular ice cream store, where she confirmed that, yes, her disguise had traveled with her.

After circling the Plaza, she turned south at La Fonda, walking several blocks to San Miguel's Chapel, touted as the oldest church in America. Massive stone buttresses anchored the adobe tower, crowned with a red-tiled roof and simple cross. Leaning against the stone wall that bordered the ancient church, as if to admire the architecture, Amanda surreptitiously dislodged a wedge-shaped rock as big as her hand, slipped in a note from her pocket for June, and then shoved the note and rock back in place. When a car sputtered behind her, she stepped back, arms crossed, gazing at the roof tiles.

Farther down the street, she turned onto the worn path along Rio Santa Fe—it made her laugh that they called this dab of water a river—where she practiced striding like a man while taking deep breaths of air so fresh it felt scrubbed. The path hugged the stream bank, bumpy with gopher mounds and wild grasses, but Amanda kept her eyes on the mountains off to the east. She was reassured by this town in which she could always see out. She loved the tidiness of the Southwestern landscape, where every rock and plant seemed to find its place. Never too much, never too little. As she strove to lengthen each step, she gazed at canyons abruptly lit by the sun. She also listened to the slap of her trousers, which sounded as loud as the bell calling fire. She was a little unnerved to be wearing slacks in public. Staring at her cowboy boots—a lucky purchase, given the need for disguise—and poking at her mustache, she took deep breaths and reassured herself again that she could pull this off. Her shorn hair had been a sign.

The idea for the disguise had been hers. June had reluctantly agreed, but only after witnessing Amanda's resolve. Yesterday evening—not even twenty-four hours ago!—June's scissors had slipped. She had been trimming Amanda's freshly washed hair after their outing to Puyé and—Amanda really should never have blurted out what she had seen between Justin and Teresa—had clipped a hunk of hair near Amanda's left temple almost to the scalp. Frantic brushing and fluffing around the bare spot had no effect; the shorn strands stuck out like mange on a cat. June, troubled by the news about Justin and clearly upset about Amanda's hair, had paced the length of the room, fist in mouth.

It was no wonder June was distraught, Amanda thought. Their history went way back. All of them—June, Justin, and Amanda—had known each other as toddlers. Justin and his father, a physician and a widower, lived next door to June's family on Santa Fe Avenue near Webber Street, a few blocks south of the Plaza. Until she was five, Amanda had lived on Don Gaspar, two blocks away. This trip to Santa Fe was Amanda's first since moving day, fifteen years ago, when she and June, hair in braids and wearing identical cotton smocks, had been tearfully separated. Letters between them had flown across the country for years. On this visit, their friendship had resumed as easily as if they still lived just blocks apart.

June's older brother, Christopher, and Justin were the same age and particular friends. They had cheerfully conspired in practical jokes on the girls, who tried to discourage them first with tearful scenes and then with quiet dignity. Neither worked. Underneath a bowl-shaped haircut, Justin's mind had raced with mischief as fast as a Stutz Speedster. And now? His blond hair was brushed back and parted down the middle. He sported two-toned shoes, straw hats, and striped blazers. And his green eyes still held laughter. After a couple of evenings, Amanda had reverted to her old habit of checking the bed for lizards. June probably did the same. She and Justin still teased each other with an easy familiarity, and Amanda knew June not only considered Justin to be her best friend but hoped someday to meet him at the altar. But despite her best efforts—and the sweetest disposition in the world, thought Amanda—June couldn't seem to interest him romantically.

So the shorn locks had been Amanda's own fault. She should have known better than to spill the beans about Justin's reaching for Teresa's hand. "Justin? With Teresa?" June had exclaimed, completely startled. Her hand had jerked up, just as she snapped the scissors shut. She had stared at the lock of hair in her hand, horrified. "Oh, Amanda!" she had cried.

"Well, I'm not sure . . ." Amanda began. "Maybe I just overreacted."

"No!" June said, holding up the lock of hair. And that's when Amanda's own brain revved into action. Frantically trying to come up with soothing words for June and at the same time looking for reassurance that it wasn't as bad as she thought, Amanda had remained in front of the mirror. Bobbed hair was still the rage, but no one had hair this short. The better to see the damage, she had put on her glasses and angled her head this way and that. When only the shorn side came into view, she had begun to laugh.

"I think I look a little like a boy," Amanda had said, turning to June who had just swung back from the window toward the dressing table. "What do you think?"

"A boy?" June had stopped in place, her brow furrowed in confusion. She was several inches shorter than Amanda, pretty but sturdy. Her tastes ran to the practical, like the hand-sewn plaid bathrobe that she wore, tied securely at her waist. "How can that help?"

"First, what do you think? Could I pass for a boy?"

Perplexed, June had looked critically at her friend's appearance. "I guess you do look a little like a boy with your hair pulled back like that, Amanda," June said.

Amanda was pleased. "Well, here's my idea. You know my quest?" Even with the horror of the situation, June had to roll her eyes. Amanda was voluble to the point of nausea on the subject of self-knowledge. "I want you to cut off the rest of my hair so I'll be in disguise! As a boy! No one will know who I really am or where I come from." She had swung back to the mirror, her eyes alight with a thrill.

"But Amanda, you're here. You're a girl! My parents will know who you are. My friends will know."

"Well, here's the crazy part," Amanda had said, glancing at June through the mirror. "Well, all right, cutting off all my hair is crazy. Here's the crazier part. After you cut my hair, I'll pack my things and write a note to your parents, saying I received a telegram from my father asking me to take the next train home. I'll say I . . ." She had glanced at the clock. " . . . took the ten forty. See? That's possible. But really, I'll stay here. Well, I mean, stay in Santa Fe. I'll leave when I planned, after Fiesta, but meanwhile I'll stay at . . . La Fonda!"

"Amanda, that's mad! Let me look at your hair again. I'm sure I can fix it. We'll find a big bow or something."

"No, June, I'm serious! This is just what I need to face those girls at Wellesley." The thought of arriving back at college, unmarried, brought a shock of terror to her heart, but her mother had made her promise to return for her junior year in exchange for this trip. "Besides, my hair will grow. Eventually. By the time I really arrive home, it will be long enough for a bob again," Amanda had said. "Or at least I'll be content to wear a hat day and night." She had looked straight at June. "And there's another thing."

"What?"

"If I stay in Santa Fe masquerading as a boy . . . and you help me . . . I can meet Justin. Get acquainted, you know? Find out what's really going on."

June's bewildered expression had switched to interest. "Really? You'd do that? For me?"

"Of course I would." While it pained Amanda that June remained unmoved by the lure of an Authentic Life, a friend was a friend. She'd do anything for her.

"You don't think he'll suspect?"

"Honestly? No. Why would he? People see what they expect to see. Besides, we haven't spent more than a few hours together. And, hmmmm . . ." She studied her round, gold eyeglasses as if for the first time. She was a little bit nearsighted. "I don't think I've ever worn my glasses when we've been out with your friends. Have I?"

"You barely wear them around this house, and you really should, you know, it's better for your eyes," June said, forgetting the crisis.

"Well, now I will. You should be happy." She continued

to study herself in the mirror. "And if I wear my hair slicked back. . . ."

"You do look different," June had said, struck by Amanda's rather stern, intellectual expression.

"So are you in? Will you cut my hair? Again?"

June looked at the scissors with trepidation. "I admit it, I'm scared."

"You'll be fine," Amanda had said. "Really, what can go wrong now? The worst that will happen is I'll be forced to join that nunnery you had your heart set on when you were eight."

June smiled and took up the scissors. "Okay then. Here goes."

They had filled out the details while June finished cutting Amanda's hair. June would dig up some of Christopher's old clothes, while Amanda wrote the note.

"What excuse will you give?" June had asked.

"I'd been thinking about a death in the family, some distant cousin or something. But then your parents would be bound to send a telegram to express their sympathy." Concentrating, Amanda had stared out at some distant, invisible spot. Then she had brightened. "What if I say my parents arrived home from Europe early and thought we could spend a few days on Martha's Vineyard before the new term starts?" Amanda had said. "Does that sound plausible?"

"I like it." June had smoothed Amanda's hair, now only two inches long. After she had parted and combed it back, one lock fell rakishly onto Amanda's forehead. June had looked at it with apprehension. "Is it all right?"

"What a handsome lad!" Amanda had said, pitching her voice down. June, laughing in relief, had put down the comb and rummaged in her desk. "Here you go," she had said, handing stationery and a pen to Amanda. "Now let's see what I can find in Christopher's closet."

Amanda had just signed her name, when June returned with an armful of clothes, smiling triumphantly and wriggling a hairy centipede.

"Oh!" Amanda had said, jumping back slightly and then recovering. "Now who's brilliant?" She stretched her hand out for the false mustache and pressed it under her nose, viewing herself in the mirror.

"I checked his box of magic tricks," June had said. "And there it was."

When Amanda had turned to face her, they had both burst into laughter. "It's perfect, Amanda," June had said. "Now hurry and get into these clothes. And let me read what you've written, so we have our stories straight." She had scanned the note. "Your apologies are positively eloquent," June smiled at her oldest friend. "And sending along the trunk is a good idea, glad you thought of it. And, you're awfully nice about what a wonderful companion I've been to you."

"Well, of course!" Amanda had said. "Now, how do I look?"

She had stood before June, transformed into a raffish young man in grey cotton slacks, grey shirt, and navy blazer. As she set a driving cap on her head, she had asked, "Hair and mustache all right?"

"You're so handsome!" June said.

"I hope you'll think about flirting with me then." Amanda had ducked her head and grinned. "I'd better be off. Don't want to be here when your parents get back from the party." She had picked up her travel bag and looked around the room to be sure she had what she needed.

"First thing in the morning, June," Amanda had continued, "I'll leave a note for you in the wall, the one you showed me, that you and Justin used in grade school?" Damn, she had thought, wincing at the pain that had swept across June's face, would she never learn? She had briefly enfolded June in a hug. "It will be all right. Everything. I promise."

June had shaken her head in misery, but finally managed to blurt, "Just in case . . . tomorrow? La Fonda's dining room? About noon?"

"I'll be there."

Amanda had started down the stairs when June called, "Wait! What's your name?"

Amanda had hesitated. Then she had tugged at the ends of her short mane and turned to give June a wry smile. "Lionel," she had said. "Lionel Hairgrove."

Lionel, she repeated to herself now, turning once more on the path. Better start thinking of herself that way. She'd be meeting June and her friends in just a little over . . . she pulled out a watch . . . two hours. Should be time enough to practice the details for her cover story. It would have to be pretty darned convincing. She not only had to persuade everyone that she *was* Lionel Hairgrove, but wrangle an acquaintance with Justin. She had just four days to do what she could to help June. A flutter of excitement mixed with her fear. Break a leg, she thought.

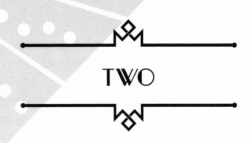

TWO

So far Lionel had not been recognized as Amanda, even though La Fonda's dining room was crowded with tourists in addition to a few churchgoing families arriving after Sunday service. Several waitresses—Harvey Girls wearing severe black-and-white uniforms—glided between tables. Lionel was seated toward the back of the dining room, partly hidden by one of the central pillars. He had the advantage of a first look at anyone entering. The initial test had been the Hendersons. Lionel had chanced to look up just as Alice was surveying the room for her lunch partners. If Alice had noticed Lionel's widened eyes—and heard his pounding heart?—she gave no notice. Spotting the painter B. J. O. Nordfeldt by the windows, Alice and her husband, Willy, passed by Lionel's table without a glance.

Since then, other friends of the Sheehans' had come and gone, with only a small town's idle curiosity about the young man reading a newspaper while finishing the last of his chicken. Lionel secretly studied the men dining nearby. He had taken so many oddities for granted. The driving cap he was borrowing from Christopher sat on the extra chair like an unexploded bomb. After earning several rebuking stares from a tableful of ladies, Lionel had finally shed it in a terror as he remembered that men never wore hats inside.

Then a new group hovered by the dining room entry. June was accompanied not only by Justin, but by Teresa and David as well. At least Lionel knew who everyone was. Would the large group make things better or worse? wondered Lionel. And how was June feeling about lunching with both Justin and Teresa?

Teresa was the girlfriend of June's brother, Christopher— they were nearly engaged, according to June—which was what had made Justin's behavior so shocking. They had been on an afternoon excursion to Puyé. June and her younger brother, Jim, had been traveling in David's car. Justin had been driving his father's car, with Teresa in front and Amanda in back. She had given up trying to converse—the car was so noisy, she'd had to shout every question or response. Instead, Amanda had leaned back to appreciate the scenery. At the time, she had been mulling over the heroic mission of pines. Just the sight of so many lonely silhouettes, practically rooted in bare rock and swinging like stickmen over cliffs, had made Amanda nearly swoon over Life's sacred burden. She had wanted to reach out and embrace the whole world, declaring, "I see your connections, though cast in the deepest of mysteries." She had felt a little giddy, as if Truth were blasting into her pores, and was sure Mabel would have felt the same. Then a movement in the corner of her eye had caused her to switch her attention from the landscape to the front seat. She had caught Justin releasing Teresa's hand, laughing as he did, then heard the words "Christopher" and "especially good care." She had no idea if Justin had tried anything during the picnic. Though now, as the group waited to be seated, it was only too plain to Lionel that Justin was putting his hand lightly on Teresa's shoulder to draw her eyes to a painting, while David leaned in to hear what Justin had to say.

David had been at the picnic, too. He had just arrived in Santa Fe to visit his mother for Fiesta. Amanda knew that David and June had been friends since high school—David at Santa Fe's public high school and June at Loretto Academy. They had met one Saturday at Santa Fe's Art Museum where, after standing together silently for a long stretch in one of the galleries, they had both admitted to being puzzled, yet captivated, by all of the strange artwork created by local artists, especially the skewed landscapes of Raymond Jonson. David was tall—six feet or more—with a firm muscled body that he handled awkwardly, as if his real self inhabited only two-thirds of it. Like Justin, he wore a lightly striped blazer and bow tie and held a driving cap in his hands. Unlike Justin, unruly brown hair framed a round face, despite the current style for slickness.

Lionel watched as June and her friends were seated at a table about midway along the west wall, away from the windows. How in the world was he going to pass casually way over there? In an attempt to scout the possibilities, he occasionally raised his eyes from the paper, as if resting them. Once he caught June's eye by mistake and both quickly cast their eyes down. Finally, Lionel made out something . . . a Pueblo pot? . . . set in a niche close to their table. That should do it.

He jotted down his room number on the check that his waitress had set on the table, taking measured breaths to calm himself. Even the theater hadn't been this nerve racking. Well, no time like the present, he thought. As he pushed back the chair, the waitress stopped for the check and flashed an enticing smile at Lionel, startling him at first, then flooding him with reassurance.

Hat in hand, Lionel threaded his way toward June and her friends. As he neared June's table, he rather ostentatiously kept his eyes on the niche . . . yes, a lovely pot . . . while managing to bump Justin's chair. He faked a stumble and then, recovering, turned toward the foursome. June and Teresa sat on either side of Justin, with David across.

"Oh, I am so sorry," Lionel said, giving a slight bow. "I'm afraid I was rather too interested in getting a good look at that pot. My apologies."

"That's all right," Justin said, glancing up. The shiny black pot, just a few inches high and about six inches wide, was graced with flat, greyish-black feathers along its rim. "Marvelous, isn't it?" he asked.

"Beautiful!" Lionel replied. "Do you know anything about it?"

"It's one of Maria and Julian's," Justin said. Lionel kept his expression blank. "The potters? From San Ildefonso? Rather famous around here, actually. They've been making that kind of pot for, what, six or seven years?" he asked, turning to the others.

"At least that long," said June. She smiled at Lionel. "New in town?"

"Passing through," said Lionel. "From Massachusetts, just north of Boston." Better to stick with something he knew, he had decided. Besides, no point in trying to tame his "r," which either regularly appeared at word endings or else entirely disappeared. "Off to California. Plan to try my luck with the movies."

"The movies!" Justin exclaimed, as he twisted to get a

better look at Lionel. It gave Lionel a start to see that his and Justin's hairstyles were exactly the same, though Justin's was blond and straight. Justin had his arm flung over the chair back and looked perfectly at ease, ready to chat up a stranger. "An actor?"

Had he already given himself away? wondered Lionel in dismay. But then he realized it would be only logical to assume he meant acting in the movies. "Scriptwriting," he quickly corrected. "Have a hundred and one ideas."

"Oh, isn't that exciting!" Teresa exclaimed, beaming at Lionel and looking to the others for agreement.

"Well, I think so," Lionel said. "Not sure the parents were too keen on the idea, but go west, young man, that's my motto."

"What kind of stories?" Justin asked.

"Mysteries, mistaken identities. That type of thing," Lionel answered. He was concentrating on keeping his voice pitched low. Better to keep his contributions short and sweet. He shifted attention back to the pot. "Is it one of a kind?"

"One of the best, I'd say, but not exactly unique," Justin answered. "You can find pots like that at traders all around town. Or at the pueblos. If you're really interested, you might look into one of Harvey's Indian Detours."

"Are you in Santa Fe for a few days?" Teresa asked. Her question rippled with Spanish rhythms, as if English were being sung. Lionel had always found her voice inexplicably soothing, and it was working its magic now. "It's nearly time for Indian Fair, when the potters will be coming to Santa Fe," she continued. "There will be lots to see then." Her face, a perfect oval, held lively acorn-brown eyes and a long, thin aristocratic nose, along with an encouraging smile, as if willing everyone to like her.

"We met potters just the other day, didn't we, David?" June said. "I was telling Justin and Teresa about our adventure." David nodded politely, but instead of responding, kept his eyes on the table's centerpiece, clearly uncomfortable.

Lionel was intimately familiar with June's reference. Amanda and June had driven home with David, because Justin and Teresa had left earlier with June's younger brother, Jim. On the way back, one short stretch of road had been turned into an unexpected quagmire from what must have been a fierce local storm. When David had tugged at the wheel to keep from sliding into a ditch, the car had responded by violently flinging itself across the mud and then settling into a set of deep ruts. David had spent at least twenty minutes shoveling and maneuvering to get them out, only to have the car find another deeper rut and die. By then, June and Amanda had joined him in the sticky gumbo, where they too were soon liberally sprinkled head to toe with a layer of brown slime, accented by huge clumps of mud that clung to the hems of their skirts. Rescue finally arrived in the form of a couple from Santa Clara Pueblo, who were driving their horse and cart, and had offered to pull them out. At the time, Amanda had thought it a great adventure, culminating in the quintessential Southwestern moment. Now, as Lionel, he could see that David hadn't felt that way at all.

"Would you care to join us?" said Justin to Lionel, glancing at the others. June joined Teresa in smiling by way of encouragement, though David continued to study the vase of daisies. "We've just ordered. I'm sure we can add a chair." Justin stood and motioned to one of the staff.

"Oh, that's very kind," said Lionel. "I just finished my

dinner, but I would enjoy a little company." He bowed slightly. "Lionel Hairgrove."

"How do you do?" Justin said. "Justin Samuels. And our lovely lady friends are June Sheehan and Teresa Gabaldon." Each smiled. "And this is David Elliot." David gave a curt nod.

"You're from Massachusetts?" Teresa said, as Lionel settled in a chair between her and David. "My fiancé . . ." She stopped and, glancing at June, blushed. "Well, I shouldn't call him that, we're not really engaged yet." She looked then at Justin, who was watching her closely. "But, anyway, Christopher—June's brother—he lives in Boston. I've always wanted to visit. It seems like a lovely place," Teresa said.

"Beautiful part of the country," Lionel said, having noticed again Justin's interest in Teresa, which bolstered his sense of purpose. He thought it was going well so far, but he'd better focus if he wanted to keep from doing anything foolish. "Always lived near water. But if I get my break in Hollywood, I'll just exchange one ocean for another, won't I?"

"Were you planning a stop in New Mexico?" David asked, rousing himself to join the conversation. His expression was sour, as if putting even eight words together was too much to ask of anyone.

"Yes, Santa Fe has such an intriguing reputation," Lionel responded. "I may spend a few days." The same waitress who had served Lionel came to the table, laden with plates. "Decided to hang around a bit," Lionel said to her, receiving another stunning smile.

"Then you'll be here for Indian Fair. That's splendid!" June said. "I think it gets better every year. Indian Fair's been around for . . . what? . . . five years maybe?" June asked.

"Since we were freshman," David remembered, a warm smile momentarily sweetening his expression.

"You'll see lots of pottery there," Justin volunteered. "And paintings. Like that one on the wall." He gestured toward the entrance. "The Pueblo woman baking bread in an outdoor oven?"

"I'll look on my way out," Lionel promised. "When is the fair?"

"Starts Tuesday," Justin said. "During Fiesta. You know about Fiesta?"

"Only since yesterday. I gather I was lucky to get a room here at La Fonda." Lionel glanced meaningfully at June. "One of the shopkeepers mentioned Fiesta to me," Lionel said. "Happens the first week of September . . . and something about costumes and dancing?"

"That's the best part," Teresa said. "And there's a parade."

"But it's much more than that," Justin said, impatient to show off his knowledge. "Fiesta is ancient. Been part of Santa Fe since the 1700s, more or less, as a celebration of Spanish conquests. It's part religious and part historic."

"And part chaos," June added. "It goes on for four days, ending with Zozobra's burning on Wednesday night."

"Zo-ZO-bra?" Lionel questioned.

"Zozobra's amazing!" Justin said. "It's Spanish, means anxiety. Some call him Old Man Gloom. He moans and groans, while we shout and string him up and burn him." His eyes were lit. "We'll set Zozobra on fire in public again this year. Will Shuster started it in his yard, and now it's part of Fiesta. The idea is that fireworks explode just as Zozobra goes up in flames, and then so do everyone's troubles."

"Don't worry," June counseled, seeing that Lionel's eyes

had widened. "Zozobra's not a person, he's a huge marionette."

"Dancing in the street starts after," Teresa added. "My cousin danced so much last year she didn't get home until two in the morning! Her mama didn't even believe her until my cousin held up her shoes—they had holes in the bottom! You shouldn't miss it."

"I know someone who's going to miss it," David said, unexpectedly. He looked directly at June. "Tell me again. Why did she have to go back east? Didn't she try to explain Fiesta to her parents?" He knew he was whining, but couldn't seem to help himself.

Lionel grew very still. What was David saying? He wasn't talking about her, was he? Lionel was pretty sure that, as Amanda, she had made it abundantly clear that attracting romance was about as welcome as finding a centipede in her shoe. Lionel's feet tapped lightly at the thought.

"Oh, David," June said. "She would love to be here. Really." She patted his hand. "But her parents wanted the whole family home. To spend time together before the new term." She spoke to the others, casually including Lionel as well. "They have a lovely place on Martha's Vineyard."

"And she'd never been to Fiesta, David," Justin added, sampling his mashed potatoes. "So she really wouldn't have had any idea what she was missing."

"I wish I'd known she was going to leave so soon," Teresa said. "I might have sent a letter back with her. Maybe even traveled with her." She spoke to June, but glanced quickly at Justin.

"To see Christopher," June added, smiling at Teresa.

"Oh, Teresa," Justin said. "You wouldn't miss Fiesta,

would you?" He reached over to lightly touch the back of her hand. Then he went back to mixing potatoes with peas, smiling brightly. "It is too bad that Amanda isn't here." Addressing Lionel, he said, "She's a longtime friend of June's, visiting from back east. Near where you come from, actually."

Lionel only nodded. He barely knew where to concentrate. On Justin's attentions to Teresa? Or David? He studied his cup of coffee.

"I'm an idiot," David said suddenly. "I'd only just met her. For what, a day?" he said to June. He groaned slightly, then looked embarrassed. "I'm so sorry," he said. "What's come over me? It's nothing. She's certainly free to spend time with her parents."

"I'm sure she'll visit again. She loved it here. She said so," June consoled. She pushed her plate to the side, glancing at the wall clock. "Teresa, look at the time, we need to skedaddle."

"Aunt Gina," Teresa explained. "It's one o'clock already?" June gestured toward the wall clock. "Oh my goodness. But we'll all see each other at the Spanish baile tomorrow?" Teresa asked, gathering up her things.

"Ab-so-lute-ly," Justin said. "And may I have a dance?" Catching June's disapproving stare, he said, "I did promise Christopher."

The group fell silent while Teresa, clearly confused, looked back and forth between June and Justin, before finally accepting.

"And may I have a dance?" David asked June, who responded with a grateful smile. Lionel relaxed at the suggestion, certain now he could stop worrying. David's feelings would soon fade. And he appreciated, on June's behalf, David's quickness. Everyone—except Justin, it seemed—knew June had been hoping that Justin would ask her first. Inviting June himself was the best David could do. He really was a good friend. According to June, she and David had tried on the idea of a crush in high school, but when her affections had stuck fast to Justin, David—painfully self-conscious in attempts at romance—had felt mainly relief at resuming a simple friendship.

"I hope we'll see you at the baile, too," Teresa said to Lionel, trying to get the conversation back to safer grounds. "It's the best party of the year, and everyone is in costume."

"A Spanish baile?" Lionel said, now feeling back in charge. He pretended confusion though he knew full well what a baile was. Amanda and June had shopped for costumes just last week.

"Oh, Teresa's absolutely right, you must come," Justin said.

"You're sure to find lots of script ideas," Teresa said.

"But . . . a costume?" Lionel said.

"You know," said June. "Christopher wore a matador's costume a couple of years ago, didn't he, Teresa?" At her nod, June continued, "I'll look for it at home. It may fit." She pretended to study Lionel, mentally comparing sizes. "If not, you could ask someone in town to make temporary alterations. Just for the night."

"If it's not too much trouble . . . ?" Lionel said. "You are too kind."

"It's settled. I'll look for it as soon as I get home," June said, tugging at her gloves. "If I can't find it, I'll send a note. Otherwise, expect it tomorrow morning at the front desk here. Er, this is where you said you were staying?"

"Yes, thank you," Lionel said, rising with David and

Justin as the girls were about to set off. He extended his hand to the girls. "Thank you again. I look forward to seeing you tomorrow evening. At the Spanish baile!"

When he sat down again with David and Justin, Lionel mentally patted himself on the back, well satisfied at how things were going. Then he steeled himself. Because if ever he was going to be found out, it was with the boys. From afar, groups of boys always seemed so competent, filled with plans to make their fortunes and change the world. He imagined conversations of import, discussions of world events, declarations of philosophical intentions. Could he keep up? But Justin's eyes on Teresa's retreating figure, a half smile hovering on his face, overpowered Lionel with an urge to make things right. Not even realizing he'd made up his mind to do so, he found himself leaning in toward the center of the table, speaking softly, "I wonder if either of you might know where I could find a drink tonight."

David shook himself from his morose meditation and looked at Lionel with some interest. Santa Fe was looser than many towns, but there was still some danger in even broaching the subject in public during Prohibition. He glanced at Justin, whose own attention had returned now that Teresa had left. "Justin?" David said, trying to ascertain how comfortable Justin might be in divulging the information.

"Lionel! A man after my own heart," Justin said, slapping Lionel on the back—who, unprepared, stifled a cough. "Actually, David and I were talking earlier about a little get-together at Hal Bynner's. He calls it tea. But no one drinks tea."

"Hal Bynner?"

"He's a poet. Real name is Witter," David said. "But everyone calls him Hal."

"Never heard of him. Should I have?"

"Only if you're a fan of that poetry stuff," Justin said. "But you don't have to like poetry to like his parties. And that's where you'll find the smartest set in Santa Fe."

"The man lives to party," David added. "Although, to be clear, we don't actually count ourselves as being in the smartest set."

"Speak for yourself," Justin said.

"But I didn't mean . . ." Lionel said, suddenly alarmed about what he'd started. "That is, I don't want to crash his party."

"Oh, it will be fine, the more the merrier," Justin said.

"Hal was friends with Justin's older cousin," David said, "and so tolerates us."

"Watch what you say," Justin said.

"Oh," said David, looking embarrassed. "I didn't mean . . ." He let the sentence drop.

Lionel was genuinely curious. "Didn't mean what?"

Justin leaned in closer. "It's not exactly talked about," he said, glancing around anyway. "But everyone in town knows. Suspects, anyway." He shrugged. "He fancies men. You know?"

"But don't worry," David said, responding to Lionel's shocked expression. "He's the soul of discretion. Really, you would never have guessed if we hadn't said anything."

Now Lionel remembered meeting Mr. Bynner at the Hendersons. David was right. He would never have guessed. With Brookline, Massachusetts, in common, Amanda and Mr. Bynner had chatted for quite a while. In fact, she had felt so at ease with Bynner's formal Boston manners, she had ended up resenting him, casting him as part of all that she was trying to reject. He was old—over forty at least—and bald. But handsome in his way. His wide, clear forehead lent him a stately air, intimating a vigorous intellect. His eyes, Lionel remembered, were secretly amused throughout their chat, as if a storyteller had been whispering wild stories about Amanda in his ear.

"Besides, he is terribly funny," said Justin. "You'll want to meet him. He knows a lot about Pueblo art. Chinese art, too. He's traveled a lot."

"Well," Lionel said, hesitantly. For a moment, he almost wished he were Amanda again, on the train, heading toward the stifling, straitlaced Brahmin culture of Boston. At least there everyone knew their place. Now, evidently, one of Amanda's own kind had somehow managed to mix up impeccable manners with what could only be imagined as a secretive, wild lifestyle. Lionel was shocked to be shocked. Before this trip, he had considered himself open minded, practically a radical when it came to liberties for all. Santa Fe's society was particularly amenable because it took you as you were. But its flexibility stemmed from its mix of cultures, and sometimes it was just plain difficult to keep up with the jumble of bohemian artists, generations-old Spanish families, and small-town American boosters. Not to mention the Pueblo Indians. And now this. It felt so complicated.

What would Mabel Dodge Luhan do? Certainly, she wouldn't dash for the nearest exit, like a scared rabbit. Lionel had better gather his wits. Give the whole of yourself to what is ahead of you, to what you want to bring to light, Lionel reminded himself. Besides, if this is where he was going to find Justin tonight, then this is where he had better go. And Mr. Bynner did have a marvelous sense of humor. He wondered if his poetry was any good. "Can't say I've ever run with that crowd before," he finally managed to answer. "But count me in."

"We can go after the procession that begins Fiesta. Why don't you meet us at about seven o'clock in front of the post office? By the cathedral? We'll watch the procession, then head to Hal's," David said.

"A religious procession?" Lionel said, this time truly baffled. "And then we're going drinking?"

"Only in Santa Fe," David said, smiling. The waitress meanwhile had placed the check on the table next to Justin. Lionel beat him to it.

"Let me," he said, sure at least about this, holding up his hand in response to Justin and David's protests. "I'm not going to argue. I'm so grateful to have met you." He stood up, shaking hands with them both. "The post office at seven. I look forward to it," he said.

THREE

"It's the lure of forbidden fruit for me," Justin said. "Irresistible." David, Justin, and Lionel—still securely disguised, or so he hoped—were lounging on the stairs that led up to Bynner's front door. Irregular pieces of limestone made up the steps, which wound almost fifteen feet around the northwest corner of the house, connecting to a courtyard encircled by an adobe wall. A tin lamp hung next to the arched wooden door that was an entrance into the courtyard, allowing them glimpses of gesturing arms and colorful gowns through the slats.

Having begun well before dark—or so it seemed—the party now filled the rambling house. By the time Lionel had arrived with Justin and David, guests were spilling from courtyards into the front yard. The house on Buena Vista was at the southern edge of town, about a mile south of the Plaza. A maid had met them at the door, leading them through a maze of crowded, compact rooms toward the back patio, where Bynner, surrounded by guests, was in the middle of telling a story. Catching sight of Justin and David, Bynner waved and pointed toward the kitchen. They had helped themselves from a table littered with bottles of various shapes and sizes, many of which smelled like whiskey. Some had labels. Most did not.

An old adobe, the house—actually two that Bynner had joined together—was a string of rooms that had been built as needed over decades, so guests pushed past each other along tiny staircases or narrow hallways leading into or out of nearly every living space. Everywhere he looked, Lionel spotted treasures—Navajo rugs covered the floor, Pueblo pots decorated the mantle, and a hand-painted red lacquer Chinese screen created a reading nook—but instead of stopping to gawk, he kept up with David and Justin, afraid of losing them in the labyrinth of rooms and crowds. Drinks in hand, guests conversed in threes and fours, serenaded by a tinny piano, a trumpet, and the high-pitched strains of Ethel Waters issuing from the Victrola. The din was incredible, punctuated by wild peals of laughter.

Most of the guests were older—their parents' age—but many knew Justin and David and stopped to shake hands. Everyone made feeble attempts to introduce Lionel, but it was impossible to hear. Finally, having inched their way into the packed courtyard, Justin pointed through the entryway to the steps, and there they had settled. Occasionally, Justin would dive back into the crowds to locate another drink or socialize. But David and Lionel agreed it was more pleasant simply to sit and sip, enjoying the mild September night. They talked little. Despite the drink, or maybe because of it, David remained wrapped in his own thoughts. Lionel felt it was not only in his own best interest to keep silent—he really feared forgetting where he was and speaking in his own voice—but he also didn't know what to say to David. A nice man, of course, and a great friend of June's. But these expressions of overwhelming love? For Amanda! Lionel felt sorry for him. He couldn't imagine ever feeling that way.

Elbows set comfortably against the wall enclosing the garden bed, filled with delphiniums and Oriental poppies, Lionel had stretched his left leg out along the step, hiding his delight in a movement so deliciously brazen. He was concentrating on trying to not fiddle with his mustache. His drink, which he sometimes managed to spill into the flowers—he thought one of the delphiniums was beginning to look as if it had had a little too much—was balanced on the garden wall. He liked drinking—one of the few things that he and Elton had enjoyed together and it gave him a pang to think so—but he preferred to stay level headed tonight. Besides the whiskey—if that's what it really was—set his throat on fire. And there was not much to cushion the alcohol—the only thing to eat was peanuts. Yet he had drunk enough to induce that dreamy calm, the chief reason he liked to drink, when the world softened with a loving light illuminating everyone, making all things seem possible.

Amid the buzz of an acre-full of conversations, Lionel reached for his glass, convinced for the moment that his host and the guests were the best examples of humankind in the world. Despite his apprehensions, the gathering was no different than any other raucous bash he'd ever attended. Of course, so far, he had barely spoken to Mr. Bynner, nor did he intend to speak to him at any length, if he could help it. He was positive Bynner would see right through the disguise. He wasn't sure if he would tell, though. Now that he was past the shock, he had begun to think of Mr. Bynner as an inspiration, a silent rebel, someone who was kin to his own aspirations of defining himself away from the crowd.

Near him, David rested his head in his hands and stared moodily at the paving stones that formed the steps. A short whiskey glass, nearly empty, listed precariously next to his right foot. Justin was stretched out on his back along the bottom step. He balanced a drink on his stomach, occasionally brushing away some pine needles and leaves that had become tangled in his coat, while his foot tapped to the rhythm of "Sweet Georgia Brown."

"Absolutely irresistible," Justin said. The noise of the party, the dark, and the alcohol had combined to inspire confidences. Remembering his mission with a start, Lionel roused himself.

"That's what you're looking for?" Lionel asked. "The thrill of the chase?" He laughed to himself. He needn't have worried about conversations of import, discussions of world events, or declarations of philosophical intentions. Apparently what boys talked about was girls.

"It excites me," Justin said.

"I don't see what's in it for you," David said. "You could have any girl. You've always been able to have any girl."

"Well, I hate to admit it," Justin said, "but you're absolutely right, David."

"There was always a gaggle of girls around him in high school," David told Lionel. "I was two years behind, so I had plenty of time to observe."

"Well, I don't see you with anyone tonight, Justin," Lionel said. "Just us boys," he added drily. "So who do you have your eye on this evening?"

Justin swung his legs and sat up. Some of his drink sloshed out of the glass. "She's not at this party. And oh, I'm in trouble," he said, leaning forward to speak more softly. "Big trouble. The best trouble."

David looked uncomfortable. "Justin, you can't really think . . ."

"But I do," Justin said. "I do think." He turned toward Lionel. "It's Teresa. I'm absolutely mad about her. She was at lunch today. On my right? Angelic face? Huge brown eyes?" His expression became dreamy and unfocused.

"I remember Teresa. But didn't she say she was engaged?" Lionel said.

"Ah yes!" Justin said. "And not just engaged . . ."

"Almost engaged . . ." David said.

"But *almost* engaged to my best friend, Christopher." In the lamp's dim light, Lionel could just make out a triumphant smile.

"Christopher is June's brother," David added. "June was at lunch, too."

"Oh, I remember June very well," Lionel said. "She seems like a girl someone could definitely become interested in. And she's not engaged." He watched for Justin's reaction.

"Oh, June," Justin said, with a warm smile but a shrug. "She's a gem. But we've known each other since her first steps. She used to tag along after Christopher and me. Everywhere. Out to the fields with our slingshots. Down to the river midsummer." He smiled fondly. "A nice girl. A very nice girl. But like a sister."

"Justin, you can't be serious about Teresa," David said. "For one, she's crazy about Christopher."

"I don't know if you've noticed," Justin said, with a self-satisfied grin, "but I'm here, and he's two thousand miles away. And there are signs she's been thinking about me."

"You're exaggerating. And even if you weren't, you

wouldn't really put your friendship with Christopher at risk?" David persisted.

"If she chooses me, well, that's really not my fault, is it?" Justin said. "Christopher's been having a good old time in Boston for two years now. I wouldn't be a bit surprised to discover he's been thinking about a girl or two himself out there."

David looked disgusted. "If you say so," he said. "You know him better. But I never had that impression of him. 'Steadfast' would be the adjective I'd use." He addressed Lionel. "June and I didn't meet until high school so I don't know Christopher as well as Justin. His and June's families were neighbors, so they go way back."

"And you and June never . . .?" Lionel asked.

"No, we've always been just friends. I think she has her eye on someone else," he said, jerking his head slightly toward Justin, who had again lain down along the steps and was gazing at the stars.

"So what are you looking for in a girl, David?" Lionel asked. "Not forbidden fruit, I guess."

Justin snorted.

"Oh, well, me . . ." David said.

"Yes. You."

"You know," he said shyly, "the first thing that attracts me in a girl is her laugh."

Justin bent his head so far back it was nearly upside down, so he could make faces at Lionel.

"That's not important to you?" Lionel said to Justin.

"I like a girl who laughs at my jokes," Justin said.

"And what else?" Lionel asked David. Meanwhile, he was madly trying to recall if he'd recently been laughing. He would have remembered to disguise it, wouldn't he? Must have, or David would have noticed.

"Oh, I don't know," David said. "Pretty face. Long legs. Slender waist. Tall." He was looking intently at the base of the chimney, which formed a portion of the house's west wall, as if it were inscribed with a portrait of his true love.

"Sounds like you have someone in mind," Lionel pressed.

David picked up his glass and drained the last mouthful of whiskey. "I just met her. But she's gone. Left unexpectedly. Before I got the chance even to say anything." He grimaced. "At least anything sensible. I just fell head over heels the moment I saw her," he said. "Could it get any cornier? Have you ever felt like that, Lionel?"

"Can't say that I have," Lionel said, reassured by the turn of this conversation. Apparently, he was in the clear. So far. "I generally take my time."

"Well, there wasn't any time. Isn't any time. I just had a day. And while I was around her, I couldn't seem to say or do anything to get her attention. And then I got her attention all right. I went and made a fool of myself, getting the car stuck, having to be rescued."

"Car stuck?" Lionel asked.

"Yesterday. Lord, it seems like a million years ago. We'd been on a picnic, a group of us, Justin, too. On the way home, June and Amanda were in my car. Then I managed to drive it right into a big old mud hole and get it stuck but good. I had to get the shovel out, place rocks, push. And I nearly had it out, too. But—can you believe it?—just as we crawled out of the first hole, the car slithered right back into another one. This time, even the girls got out to help. They were covered in mud in no time. I cringe every time I think of it. And then the Indians from Santa Clara came along. Good news, sort of. The man, Alfonso, ended up hitching his horses to the car and pulling us out." He sighed. "I was so grateful to get that car back on the road, but I did feel even more like a fool. Horses!"

"And, what, you think the girl left town because you got the car stuck in the mud?"

"Oh, no," David said miserably. "She was expecting to stay in Santa Fe for Fiesta. That's what June said, anyway. Amanda had been visiting June's family. But her parents—out east—cabled her to come home."

Justin, bored by David's confession, sat up and punched Lionel lightly on the knee.

"Enough about David," Justin said. "What about you? What attracts you?"

Lionel hitched both elbows back onto the garden wall, closed his eyes, and thought for a minute. "I don't have a type, really. But I am attracted to a girl who really knows herself," he finally said. "Someone who seems curious about life, but not chasing after every little thing that comes along. I like a girl that's serious and lighthearted both. Know what I'm saying?"

David and Justin stared at Lionel, openmouthed. Then Justin began to laugh. "That is the dumbest thing I have ever heard any fellow say." His grin was wide. "Is that how you boys talk out east?"

"Seriously, Lionel," David said, "what's in that drink? We're talking girls, here, Lionel. Sweet-tempered, bright-eyed, happy-go-lucky girls." Though to be honest, it had just occurred to him that Lionel's description was exactly what he had in mind. But, with Justin laughing, he didn't want to say so.

"Heh-heh," Lionel managed. "Almost had you, didn't I? Wanted to see if you were listening." He yawned, cursing himself. At least the darkness gave him room to recover.

Around the front yard, partygoers kept rearranging themselves into new groups, while laughter from each cluster had begun to verge on the hysterical. "How long do these parties go on, anyway?" he asked. He thought it must be two in the morning, at least.

"Until the wee hours," Justin said.

"Hal usually goes to bed when everyone leaves. At least three, or later."

"Sleeps until noon, works a little, and then does it all over again," Justin added. "He does travel a lot, but he's always in town for Fiesta."

"What a life, eh?" Lionel said. He stood up, feeling light headed despite his care in nursing the drink. "I hate to spoil a party, but I think I should be finding my way back to the hotel now. But thank you for taking me along. Enjoyed it." He looked across the property toward the road. "Which way is La Fonda?"

"I'll get you going in the right direction," David said, standing up and brushing off the seat of his pants. "In fact, I think I'll head on home myself. Justin?"

"You go ahead," Justin said. "I'll stay awhile."

"Forbidden fruit?" Lionel asked.

"Maybe," Justin said, lifting his head to give the front yard a quick survey, then returning his gaze to the stars.

Unable to ignore twenty years of etiquette, Lionel walked back into the house to say good night to Mr. Bynner, David following behind. He'd make it quick. In the parlor with the Victrola, several guests lounged on the sofa or sat on the floor, staring at two couples dancing. In the dining room, a spirited, drunken conversation had erupted among those who crowded around the table, eating peanuts. Lionel finally located Hal in the small patio behind the kitchen, where he and others had arranged themselves on chairs or wooden boxes—whatever they could find—to watch a slim man about Lionel's age, book in hand, acting out some kind of play. He wasn't dressed for the part—he was wearing white trousers and a V-neck sweater with the sleeves pushed up, showing off tanned, attractive arms. Lionel, intrigued by the spectacle, motioned to David and slipped into the patio's shadows. The young man had pitched his voice high, like a woman's.

> You may go now, no, I want something,
> I want some cake, no, not cake, bread with raisins,
> No, not bread with raisins—what it is I want?

The young man then swiveled and, assuming a lower tone, declared, "You were about to invite experience."

The impromptu audience laughed. Alice Henderson, next to Hal, grinned at him as if he had accomplished something both wicked and clever. Hal touched her arm in response, but his eyes, bright, remained fixed on the actor, who was continuing in a high voice:

> I am a lady who has never cared,
> I have had everything,
> I was born in a rich man's pocket
> Of his wedding ring,
> I am not a lady of autumn
> But a lady of spring
> Who has never really experienced
> Anything.
> I desire to know what life is like
> What the days and nights may bring,

So please do all that you can for one
Who has met the British King.
My Chamberlain has taken down
Exactly what I have said.
I want to buy experience.
Dictated, but not read.

From his place in the corner, Lionel watched Hal absently drawing circles on his glass with his right thumb. Despite the hour, he looked dapper, a gold silk tie tucked into a dark shirt. Lionel thought he seemed a little off balance, though, as if the choice of entertainment had been taken out of his hands, and he wondered about the actor and the play. But Hal's smile appeared unerasable and—how could he even know this?—even his skin seemed to smolder. He radiated elation like a weary traveler who had just glimpsed the light of home. Lionel studied the actor again and then, taking another look at Hal, it struck him: he was looking at a man, madly, deeply, and truly in love.

He nudged David and stuck his thumb toward the door. Etiquette be damned.

They walked away from the property and along the road, saying little. Shaken by the sight of Hal, Lionel wondered whether he had ever understood anything at all about love. When he had vowed to turn his back on it, had he realized he was saying no to a feeling like that? Replaying that moment, Hal seemed to shimmer in a sphere of light, while the rest of the audience shrank into weathered, tattered grey.

"Who was that man, do you know?" he asked.

"In the patio, reading from Bynner's new play?"

"I guess. Wait, that was Bynner's play?"

"It's called *Cake*. Saw a copy at my mother's. It's causing a bit of a fuss, actually, because it's Hal's portrait of Mabel Dodge Luhan. And not very flattering. But terribly funny, don't you think?"

"Mabel Dodge Luhan!"

"She lives in Taos, one of the movers and . . ."

"Yes, I know who she is," Lionel said, more sharply than intended, but David appeared deaf to anyone's emotions but his own tonight. Mr. Bynner poking fun at Mabel, Lionel's light in the desert! The depth of his fury surprised him. Bewildered by this first glimpse of true love, now fuming at its messenger, angry words hurtled around Lionel's brain, forming phrases he wanted to spit in disgust. But he caught himself—a rant against *Cake* was surely the last thing anyone would expect of him. If he intended to continue this masquerade, he needed to calm down and return to facts. "And the man, is he a friend of Hal's?" he asked, still detecting his own snippy tone, despite the aim for composure.

"Might be Hal's houseguest, Bob Hunt."

May their love rot in hell, Lionel thought. The image of Mabel as a figure of jest in Hal's hands made him livid. Hal had no right! Hopefully his moment of bliss would be not only short lived but followed by a slow, agonizing lesson in unrequited love. Now crowding the recent portrait of Hal in love were its diseased manifestations—Elton's betrayal, June's confusion, Justin's conceit, even David's sulks. He stole a glance at his companion and felt his fury and confusion over Hal encompass David as well. Here he was, striding along beside him, well within Lionel's power to take him aside and tell him in no uncertain terms that he was making himself miserable over an illusion. Well, maybe he would.

"So what part of town do you live in?" Lionel asked. He marveled at his own voice, forming questions, because his mind still reeled with a welter of angry reactions.

"Over there," David said, pointing to the right. "My mother's house is off Canyon Road. A lot of artists live near there. Though I'm just up here for Fiesta. I'm studying architecture at the university in Albuquerque." In high school, David had lived in Santa Fe with his mother, while his father remained with David's two older sisters at their home near Chicago. The official reason for the separation was his mother's health and his father's need to manage the Chicago office. But having watched his parents' icy, formal relationship for over twenty years, David could tell a different story.

"Someone in your family is an artist?"

"Not exactly. But my mother sketches. Landscapes, still lifes. She always makes portraits for family birthdays."

"Still?" Lionel said.

"I have one for each year since I was a baby," David said. "Kind of embarrassing. But I have to say she's pretty good. Even if she is my mother."

Crossing the road, they were careful to stay out of the way of an automobile weaving from one side of Manhattan Street to the other. Farther down, the unsteady driver honked at a group on the sidewalk and let out a cheer.

"Is that why you went into architecture, do you think?" Lionel asked, even as one part of his brain still considered reading the riot act to David. "Do you have some of your mother's artistic talent?"

"Maybe," David said. "And my father's an engineer. So it does seem a happy combination. And I'm definitely intrigued by the possibilities. There's an architect in town,

John Meem? His work is wonderful. He's going to remodel La Fonda for Fred Harvey."

"La Fonda? Really? That's impressive. And you're hoping to work with him someday?"

"If I'm lucky."

"Oh, I bet you are."

David kicked at a stone. It rattled up the road ahead of them. "Oh, I don't know if I'd say I was lucky." After several minutes, with Lionel still inwardly fuming, David said, "What would you do?"

"What do you mean?" Lionel asked, startled.

"About the girl I just met. Amanda. What would you do? Should I just forget her? Or do you think I should talk to June? Maybe I could write her, or something?"

"Hmm . . . writing," Lionel said. Much less drastic than grabbing David by the arm and lambasting him about love in general and Amanda in particular. And it might be easier—if slightly less satisfying—to explain everything to David in a reply. It was a pity, too, that David didn't seem to know anything about Mabel's brilliance. He could tell David when he wrote. Get him to see the light. Meanwhile, it would keep Lionel's disguise intact and give him some time to cool down. "There's an idea. It would give you a chance, anyway. See if she's interested. If not, well, you'd know, wouldn't you? And then it would be easier to forget her."

"Since I met her, I feel like I'm composing letters in my head to her all the time," David said, ignoring the notion that Amanda's reply might be *Not Interested*. "It would be a relief to get one down on paper." They were passing Loretta Academy, heading down the last block before La Fonda. "But what if I say something stupid? That would be worse."

"Look, if you're really worried, I could take a look before you send it." Lionel felt like a ventriloquist had taken over.

"Would you?" David said. "That would be swell." They had arrived at the hotel. "This whole thing is kind of awkward. I know we've just met, but I trust you." He sighed. "Just talking with boys is easy, you know? It's around girls, I get all tongue tied."

"Maybe you should see what June thinks though," Lionel suggested, backpedaling slightly at David's anxious, lovelorn face. "If you and she agree it's a good idea, then drop by La Fonda. You can leave a copy at the front desk, if I'm not around. I'll be in town a day or two at least."

"You still thinking about coming to the baile tomorrow?"

"If I can get a costume. Remind June when you talk with her, all right?"

"Sure." His tone was lighter than it had been all day, and he seemed visibly cheered by the idea of communicating to his lost love. Lionel watched him strike off toward Canyon Road.

Instead of entering La Fonda, Lionel stepped into the light of a lamppost where he scribbled a note on a small, torn sheet of paper that he had pulled from his pants pocket. He was still angry at Mr. Bynner, and the conversation with David had created its own ball of confusion in his brain, but hopefully he'd sort it out in the clear light of morning. In the meantime, he had to attend to his primary mission. He walked back three blocks to San Miguel where, jiggling the loose rock in the wall, he caught a slip of paper about to fall out. "Am miserable! What did you find out? Parents completely bamboozled. Love the mustache." Lionel laughed and then, startled by its cheerful sound, scribbled a postscript on his own note: "Less like sister, more like forbidden fruit. Will explain, meet at 1, LF lobby. PS: Say yes to letter."

FOUR

June balanced a parcel, bound with brown paper and string, on top of the stone wall in front of San Miguel's. The package held Christopher's matador costume, which she had promised Amanda. Well, Lionel. June pulled her purse open and appeared to rummage in it. It was early, not even seven o'clock, and the streets around the church were quiet. Last night's revelers had staggered home by now, and it was not yet time for the civic groups to be out and about for today's events. Her own family—June, her parents, and her younger brother, Jim—had celebrated last night at the Kelly's, arriving home well after midnight. When she left the house this morning, they were asleep. The only visitors at San Miguel's were a flock of chickadees chattering in the locust tree and one hummingbird sticking its needlelike beak into a flowering purple sage. But just in case, she was trying to give the impression that she had stopped to look for something. As she held her purse with one hand, she jiggled the rock with the other, saw a slip of paper, and tugged.

She dropped the note in her purse while shoving the rock back. Then pawing through her purse again, she pulled out the paper as if this is what she had been looking for all along. Her heart was pounding with such force, she might as well have been doing something illegal. Honestly, she reminded herself, no matter what Lionel had discovered, it was hardly a matter of life and death. But it could affect a lifetime of happiness, she told herself, before grimacing at such drama. That was Lionel's department. "Less like a sister," she read. "More like forbidden fruit."

"What the dickens does that mean?" she muttered. Only with her disappointment did she realize how much she'd been hoping to discover, well, she didn't really know what. That Justin was in love with her after all? How foolish could she be? A sister, eh? That's how he thought of her? Though why should that surprise her? Their easygoing friendship was one of the best things about him. Even in high school, while captivating one girl after another, he still sought out June to talk. About anything. About everything. They'd bicker about who was the better author, Henry James or Edith Wharton. F. Scott Fitzgerald or that new writer Justin liked so well, Ernest something. Or movie actors, Keaton versus Chaplin. She would be his friendly ear after arguments with his father. He'd dole out advice about the best subjects for her to take in school.

So being friends was getting in the way? Is that what Amanda meant? Thank goodness she had named a time and place to meet. Too bad it was nearly five hours from now. She'd be twisting and turning Amanda's words every which way until then. And, "say yes to letter"? Really. What letter? Was she supposed to write Justin? She had no idea. Amanda was a dear but needed to learn a thing or two about notes.

June snapped her purse shut and picked up the parcel. As she walked toward La Fonda, she mulled over Amanda's words. More like forbidden fruit. She imagined Adam, naked but looking remarkably like Justin, gazing at her while holding out an apple.

Amanda's eyes were like slits. She tried to coax them open to check out her reflection in the mirror. It was noon—she planned to meet June in an hour and wanted to grab a bite of something before then. She didn't feel all that clear-headed. She'd been awakened at eleven by the triumphant entry of De Vargas and the Spaniards into the plaza. For a few minutes, she'd heard a cheerful rumble of sounds from the Fiesta crowd, but then she fell back asleep. At noon, she had woken again with a start. This time, she felt upset about something and was trying to remember what.

Slowly, the evening's emotions surfaced. Now she recalled finding out about Bynner's farce about Mabel. The nerve! It made her want to scream. And she was also irritated with David. She couldn't remember the details. Probably for his naïve belief that love—Amanda's love!—would make him happy. It made Amanda want to shake him. Wait, was there something about a letter? But her aching head discouraged any further attempts to unravel last night's happenings.

She decided to concentrate on the practical. She rinsed out some of her underthings, now laying about the room. Lord knows what the maids would think. Then she tidied her few clothes, brushing the pants and blazer, spot cleaning the collar and tie. Hair slicked back and chin in hand, the face of Lionel stared back from the mirror. Short hair definitely had its advantages. Lionel was even growing used to the glasses.

He had better get going. At the door, his fingertips brushed automatically against his upper lip. He gasped. Where was it? He'd practically been asleep before he'd undressed, despite—or maybe because of—his ragged state. He shook out blankets and pillows until finally the mustache sailed, like a propeller seed, from the folds of the pillowcase. One end was crumpled. He carried the mustache back to the mirror and laid on a thick line of spirit gum to fix the bent end in place. By the time he left the room, he was breathing fast.

In the lobby, the clerk called out, "Mr. Hairgrove!" He motioned him to the desk. "This came for you early this morning," he said, pulling out a brown parcel and handing it to Lionel. "A young lady dropped it off."

The matador costume. He'd forgotten. "Thank you so much," he said, glancing at the wall clock. Quarter to one. So much for that bite to eat. He needed to try on the costume. If it didn't fit, June would know what to do. Back in the room, he tore open the package, dropping the pants, stockings, bolero jacket, and hat onto the bed. June had even included a pair of black slippers. Bless you, Lionel thought. Otherwise, Señor Matador would have shown up in cowboy boots. Undressing quickly, he pulled on the knee-length pants—big in the waist but all right otherwise—and the bolero jacket, which was plenty large enough to hide suspenders. A quick look in the mirror satisfied him. He left the costume scattered on the bed—now the maids really would have something to think about—hurriedly dressed, and checked his mustache . . . twice. By the time he entered the lobby, June was walking in the entrance.

"Why, it's Miss Sheehan, isn't it?" Lionel said, slightly

out of breath. "I received your package this morning. So very kind of you."

"How nice to see you again, Mr. Hairgrove. And the costume? Will it be suitable, do you think?"

"Made my blood rush as soon as soon I put it on. I sort of hoped a bull might come charging out of the closet." June laughed. "I wonder," Lionel went on, "would you have a few minutes? The costume could use a little tuck in the waist. Maybe we could take a stroll around the Plaza, and you could advise me on how I might get that taken care of? If I'm not taking you away from something?"

"A walk sounds perfect. I've just come from the DeVargas Day pageant."

Lionel stepped ahead to hold open the door for June, who walked through it, whispering, "What moves! You're a natural."

The street noise hadn't prepared Lionel for the hordes of people gathering across the way in the Plaza. "Oh dear," he said to June. Friends called out to each other, guitarists strolled among them, and a long line of customers waited for lemonade from the Women's Board of Trade stands. "I completely forgot about the pageant. Was it good? I really meant to go. But we were out so late last night."

June laughed. "Now you know Fiesta. You'd better get with it! Besides, the best is yet to come."

"David, Justin, and I went to Hal Bynner's," Lionel said. "He had sort of a Fiesta opening party last night. Though I gather he finds some excuse for having a party as often as possible no matter what time of year. It must have been after two by the time I got back to the hotel. But you got my note obviously. I hope it made sense."

"Not much, my dear. 'More like forbidden fruit.' Are we talking mangoes?"

Lionel laughed. "I thought you would wonder." He started toward the Plaza, but June placed a hand on his arm.

"You know, everyone's in the Plaza. We'll be bumping into people I know, right and left. Let's walk toward the river, all right?"

"Fine by me. And I'll do my best to explain. But I'm starving to death. Do you think Kaune's would be open?"

"We can try," June answered. "But talk while we walk. Don't wait."

Faced with forming an explanation, the import of last night's events came rushing back: the conversation with Justin, then Lionel's insight about Hal being in love, his wonder at feeling a love so strong, then finally his discovery of Hal's mistreatment of Mabel, which had somehow twisted itself into fury at David's impossible crush on Amanda. Where to begin? Better focus on Justin. "First, he does like you," Lionel began. "But not that way?" Lionel wondered how to express the problem without hurting June's feelings. Remembering Justin's smug proclamations about Teresa, he added, "June . . . are you sure you want to hear exactly what he said?"

June turned in alarm. "Why? What happened?"

"It's just . . ." Lionel drew in a deep breath, stopping to face June. "You know what I suspected after driving with Justin and Teresa to the picnic. That he has his eye on Teresa?" June kept her eyes on Lionel and nodded. "Well, I wasn't wrong. He made that clear last night. But it's for the silliest of reasons," he said quickly, hoping to ease June's distress. "He's one of those fellows who likes the thrill of the chase."

"Oh!" June said, a bit relieved at the truth, but irritated by the banality of Justin's motivations. "I suppose I should have understood that by now." Her eyes darkened. "And so that's what you meant by forbidden fruit?"

"I mean I'm sure he really does like Teresa. But it's not real love," Lionel said, then stopped, taken aback by his memory of Hal. "You know what I mean. He's just being stupid. I don't mean he's evil or anything."

"Evil!" June exclaimed. "Well, of course not." But she looked dismayed.

"It's just one of those brainless things boys do," Lionel said. "Like getting into fights or firing off guns." He paused. "I do like him, June." When June glanced up sharply, Lionel quickly amended, "Oh no, of course not, not like that. I just meant that, even though he was making these ridiculously arrogant pronouncements all evening, I still felt his charm. He can be terribly funny. Just because he's acting like a horse's ass doesn't mean I don't understand the attraction."

"Oh, this is awful," June said. "Maybe it was better not knowing. I should just give up."

"Now is not the time, June," Lionel said. "We know what he wants."

"Yes," June replied sharply. "Teresa. And—clearly—not me."

"Ah, but it could be you. He likes you. I'm sure of it. But, like a chump, he takes you for granted. We can fix that, you know. Make it clear you're interested in someone else. I was thinking about . . . maybe David?" Actually, Lionel hadn't been thinking along these lines at all. But now that he'd said it, the suggestion struck him as positively brilliant. He had been silly to feel so aggravated by David. Probably just taking out his anger on the nearest object, which happened to be him. Having a crush wasn't a crime. But it wasn't doing David any good, was it? Lionel thought he saw a way for both David and June to profit from the plan. June paying

David attention now might be just what the doctor ordered. Who knew? If Justin didn't come around, maybe the timing would be right, and June and David could fall in love.

"Who's to say David would be interested in my being interested?" June asked, turning the corner at San Francisco Street. "And, anyway, I wouldn't want to mislead David. Isn't that what we're irritated with Justin about?"

"Well, this is kind of embarrassing for me to admit. But David did tend to go on and on about me. Me, Amanda, I mean. Not me, Lionel." They were approaching Kaune's. "You saw how he was in the restaurant. He was even worse last night. If you would just give him a listening ear, I think he'll be more than attentive to you. And there's no reason you can't be clear about why. He'll want to help, especially in the cause of unrequited love."

"Oh, Amanda," June said, as they drew up to the shop door. "I should have told you when we got home from the picnic. I knew David liked you. He told me so." In fact, June was responsible for David even being in Santa Fe. With little experience but much hope, she had decided to try her hand at matchmaking. She had written to David about Amanda and encouraged him to visit Santa Fe during Fiesta. Knowing Amanda as well as she did, she had said nothing at all to her. But now look.

"He'll get over it," Lionel said drily. "Although it does seem like he's more than willing to carry a torch. In fact, he said he was going to ask if you thought it would be a good idea to write me."

"He already did. Talk to me, I mean. He called at the house this morning. And I said yes. Well, I might have said yes, anyway, but I *strongly* encouraged him after getting your note. That's what you meant in your PS? 'Say yes to letter'?"

"Exactly! Thank you." This might work out very well. Now Lionel could freely write back, letting David down easy while pointing him to a way to really experience life.

"Well, I think that's sweet of you. But, if you don't have feelings for him, shouldn't you be trying to discourage him?"

"I will. That's the point. When I write, I'll gently explain, and then he can get on with his life. Except, oh!" Now Lionel remembered why he had added the postscript. "Just before we parted last night, I did offer, if you thought writing would be all right, to read his letter before he sent it to be sure he wasn't saying anything stupid."

"You what?" June stopped again and stared at her friend.

"Well, what difference will it make if I read it now?" Lionel said defensively. "It will give me a chance to see what he's thinking so I can find the best way to discourage him. Better sooner than later, don't you think?"

June looked incredulous, but they cut their conversation short as they peered into the windows of the shop, one of only a small number of stores open for a few hours during Fiesta. With so many opportunities to be overheard, they chatted about DeVargas Days while waiting in line to purchase a roll and an apple for Lionel. June said this morning's pageant had been exactly the same as it had been every year, but its consistency was a comfort. Still talking as they left, Lionel stepped out of the shop directly in front of Justin who was forced to stop abruptly, barely avoiding being shoved into the street.

"Blast!" Lionel said, when he saw what he had done. "Oh, dear. Oh, Justin! You must forgive me. I am such a bumbling, shuffling fool these days." He shifted the food to his left hand and held out his right to shake. "I seem to take the phrase 'run into someone' quite literally."

June laughed. "Justin," she said. "How wonderful to see you. Isn't this the best time of year? And guess what? Lionel has said he's coming to the grand ball! He's wearing Christopher's matador costume and will look smashing, I think." Rushing her words, she said to Lionel, "I'm sure if you leave the costume at the front desk they can take it in that inch or so you mentioned."

"I'll do that," Lionel assured her. "Did you stay long after we left?" Lionel asked Justin.

"Maybe an hour," Justin said, looking from one to the other. Well, well, he thought. "We went to Hal's last night," he told June.

"Heard all about it," June said. "Lionel and I met in line. Mother needed something from Kaune's. That Hal. He's always good for a party, isn't he? Anyone I know there?"

"Not too many from our old crowd," Justin said. "The Fergusons were at the party. In fact, they were still there when I left at about three."

"And here you are, all bright and shiny." Lionel said. "I just barely got out of bed." He pointed to the roll and apple. "This is breakfast."

"Just woke up myself," Justin said. "The office is closed because of Fiesta, but my boss asked if I'd finish up some paperwork. That's where I'm headed."

"Did you see my note? I left it on your door." June asked. "My parents invited some friends to our house before the baile. They told me to invite mine, too."

"Yes, thank you," Justin said.

"We can expect you then? About eight thirty? My little brother is inviting friends, too. And David said he'd come. Teresa, too." June slightly stuttered her name.

"Wouldn't miss it," Justin said, his sudden eagerness not lost on either June or Lionel.

"And Lionel, of course!" June said. "You will be able to join us? I left a message with the costume."

"Oh, I'm so sorry," Lionel said, somewhat taken aback. "I'm afraid I didn't notice the invitation." He looked helplessly at June, who managed to keep a neutral expression. He couldn't imagine that June expected him to go. The Sheehans would see through the disguise in seconds. He began to babble. "I would love to, naturally, but on the train here I made the acquaintance of a professor and his wife. History. Professor Darnelle. When I ran into them— no, not literally this time—yesterday afternoon, they kindly invited me to have dinner with them at the hotel. I'm so sorry. Please give your parents my regrets."

"Oh, that's too bad. But we'll look forward to seeing you at the baile, then," June said, visibly relaxing at Lionel's response. "We're all going to meet outside the entrance. About ten thirty." She included Justin in her glance.

"I'll be there," Lionel said. Finishing the roll, he brushed crumbs onto the street, then shook hands with Justin. "So nice to see you," he said. "But I need to get that costume altered."

"We'll watch for you at the baile then," Justin said, before turning to June. "Walk with me to my office?"

About to say yes, June instead shot a quick glance at Lionel. "So sorry, Justin," she said. "I told Mother I'd check on Aunt Gina. She was feeling poorly yesterday when Teresa and I stopped by." She leaned forward to accept a kiss on her cheek, then turned to Lionel. "I hope you'll enjoy your day, Mr. Hairgrove. I look forward to seeing you tonight."

FIVE

A manda left La Fonda in the late afternoon and set off toward the foothills to the east. Fiesta Theater was a good mile away, yet she could hear the faint pounding of drums as she walked toward Canyon Road. She was sorry to miss the Indian dances—everyone tonight would be asking Lionel if he had gone—but according to the program in the newspaper, there'd be another chance tomorrow. She didn't feel up to masquerading this afternoon—her head still ached slightly—so her choices were either to hole up in her room or hike away from town. Fresh air seemed like the better cure and, so far, she was enjoying the solitary ramble. Just blocks from the Plaza, yet here was country, with fields and orchards sheltering sprawling adobe homes. Trees lined the road, vigas sprouted from roofs, and uneven adobe walls that looked likely to crumble with the first good rain marked property lines. The road itself was a bumpy web of shoe prints, paw prints, and hoof marks left in the mud after the evening rains. Caked mud covered everything—gate latches, low bushes, the wooden slats that served as a sidewalk. Amanda could hear hens squabbling and the bleat of sheep. She thought she remembered Teresa saying that her mother's family, the Vigils, lived out here somewhere. Didn't some of the artists live back here, too? Five little nuts in adobe huts, as they were known around town—Will Shuster, Fremont Ellis, and the others.

But Amanda wasn't planning a visit. She was aiming for the mountains. She supposed, as a city girl, she ought to be afraid of being on her own in this kind of country. Instead she felt exhilarated, enjoying a boy's freedom. Here was authenticity! Ahead, grey-green piñon and crooked cedar trees coated the ridges and spread into shadowed canyons. Immense jagged rocks, piled high and catching the sun, jutted out from parts of the hillside like secrets brought to light. Crows circled above—occasionally a hawk. The brilliance of the sky, the grandeur of the hills made Amanda feel so alive, it practically hurt. She wanted to find a trail where she could enjoy the moment, wander, and think. She had a lot on her mind.

So far, the disguise had been a success. She hadn't slipped up—as far as she knew—and her foray into intelligence gathering had paid off. June's decision to say no to Justin this morning proved it. And she felt good about the David plan, too—it was tidy and humane. Besides, if he wanted the sweetest girl in the world, he really should pursue June. Take that, Justin. She fingered David's letter, tucked into her pocket, which David had dropped at La Fonda. She hadn't had time to read it yet, but regardless of its contents, she knew she would encourage him to mail it. There'd be plenty of time to construct an answer.

Even after their chat last night, it seemed remarkable to her that he could harbor such a crush. Daydreaming about dates and kisses, wedding gowns and cakes . . . it seemed a lifetime ago. She had spent just the one afternoon with David, along with June and her friends, picnicking not far from the ruins of Puyé. Frankly, Amanda hadn't paid much attention. He seemed nice enough, but what she remembered best about their day was the landscape. The way the New Mexico sky filled every view, relegating objects on earth to second place. The cliff rooms that archaeologists had uncovered. And the pottery sherds she'd found in one of the clearings. Off by herself, she had tried to commune with the ancient ones who had touched such things, immersing herself in the vast continuum of time . . . life was her passion, not some dead-end scheme for love. Though, suddenly, the memory of Hal's expression surfaced, a tantalizing blend of contentment and thrill. She shook her head as if to flick the image into the forest.

And the couple from Santa Clara . . . the excitement of meeting Alfonso and Serafina! That was the high point of her day. How kind they'd been to stop and help. Yet yesterday at lunch, David seemed only in an agony of embarrassment over the stalled car. She was sorry he couldn't feel her own clarity of purpose, which freed her from such muddles. In her reply, she would make sure to be a guide, like Mabel. The thought sent her shoulders back, head up.

Yes, it was a pity about David. He would be better off questing for self-knowledge rather than moping over girls, especially her. She would read the letter, politely steer him away from thoughts of her, and clue him in on the real value of life.

If only dealing with Mr. Bynner's offense could be as easy. The thought of his publishing a whole book designed to make fun of Mabel made Amanda's chest tighten as if a roar of anger circled her heart. What right had he to injure Mabel's reputation? Didn't he understand that she had demonstrated extraordinary courage in pulling away society's curtain so that Life was on display? Wouldn't you think that he, of all people, would champion, not throttle, such a defender of Truth? And after all of Amanda's pains yesterday to finally come to peace with his inexplicable preference for men . . . she had started to admire him as a secret rebel . . . well, she might as well have saved herself the effort. He must be a petty man after all if he was manufacturing laughs at Mabel's expense. Just knowing that he was going about his day as if nothing had happened . . . it made her so furious, she could hardly see.

She came to a halt, fuming, evergreens thick around her. The road she'd been following had dwindled to a footpath, and she had hiked high enough to look down on Santa Fe. There was the cathedral with its unfinished spire, a tiny spot in a vast setting. Near there, Mr. Bynner was pleasantly engaged, wrecking lives. Amanda couldn't stand by and watch. She practically owed Mabel her life. She must make Hal pay.

The problem was, how? Amanda set off again, heading toward a limestone outcrop not too far away, running possibilities through her mind. She'd like to take care of it personally and, preferably, before she left Santa Fe. She wanted to see the effects herself and not have to depend on June for reports. Should she take June into her confidence? Recruiting a partner was tempting, but it could complicate more than help, and she wasn't sure June would be interested. June would do anything for her, she knew, but even June thought Amanda's allegiance to Mabel was vastly out of proportion. Disappointed, Amanda had chalked it up to timing, believing that, someday, June would understand. So she'd better do this on her own.

But what? Something she could do herself and quickly. Bynner's crime seemed so heinous that, as far as she was concerned, all limits were off. She just had to decide on the easiest way. There was his lifestyle, of course. If she were still in Boston, she'd only have to spread a rumor or two. But if Justin's and David's attitudes were anything to go by, hints of homosexuality weren't likely to have much effect here. Santa Fe already knew and it didn't seem to matter.

Something else, then. What other things did he care deeply about? Justin had mentioned Hal was a keen collector of art—maybe there was something there? She envisioned a roomful of cracked pots and stained rugs, but the sight made her feel worse, not better. Vandalism was out apparently, or at least her sense of aesthetics seemed to think so. What else?

Hints of art fakery? That seemed closer to what she had in mind except for one thing—she knew practically nothing about art. She didn't think Wellesley's Introduction to European Art qualified. If she didn't know enough to convince herself, how could she persuade anyone else? And no time for research, either. She thought the idea had possibilities, though. She'd revisit it if nothing better came along.

Attack the source—*Cake*? Write a scathing review? There's an eye for an eye, she decided, quickly testing out phrases: "completely out of touch," "oblivious of Mrs. Luhan's genius," "rhythmic nightmare." And she'd only heard a few lines from his play! She warmed to the idea. She would have to find a publisher, maybe the *New Mexican*? Its editor might be open to publishing a review from a Santa Fe visitor . . . she could provide Lionel with a few fake credits from a couple of Boston papers. Her uncle's articles were always on the editorial page of the *Globe*. She could offer his name as a reference, create a literary background for Lionel, a man who had studied . . .

A man! She'd nearly forgotten Lionel. And who was Hal interested in? Men. Surely there was something she could do with that. Hal's lovelorn expression resurfaced and, this time, Amanda smiled. How would Hal feel if he suddenly had a rival for Bob Hunt's affections? Someone like . . . Lionel. Ha. Now she was on to something. She liked it. It had everything she needed: it struck close to Hal's heart, she could accomplish it on her own, and she would be able to get started quickly. Tonight even, at the baile. She'd keep it simple: make friends with Bob, encourage him to leave the baile with her—for an hour, at least—and be sure Hal saw them. Jealousy should do the rest.

At the outcrop, which loomed above her, she scrambled up about twenty feet, pushing away shrubs and ducking under pine limbs. Dry needles stabbed her palms, but she barely felt them. Make Hal jealous. Perfect. She hoisted herself up onto slabs stacked like giant blocks, then stood and surveyed the view before jumping across a narrow crevasse onto a bordering slab. She settled on the boulder at the edge of the formation, feet dangling over the drop.

Lionel and Bob Hunt. Beautiful. She'd need to work out the details, but she would have time for that on her hike back to town. She'd better move on to her next problem: David.

She pulled his letter from her pocket, ideas about the Bob Hunt plan still churning. She was reluctant to let go, images of getting to know Bob Hunt among a set of costumes, band music, and darkness skittering through her mind. Should she skip David's letter? She suspected its contents would basically be a rehash of everything she'd already heard: love at first sight, apologies for the stuck car, a promise of enduring devotion. As if she would ever believe that. She contemplated the envelope. Maybe she should just tuck it back into her pocket or, better yet, pitch it. When they met at the baile, she could simply tell him she'd done him a favor and burned it. Give up, she'd say. Love at first sight is all in your head. And certainly not reciprocated. Amanda was not interested, is not interested, will not be interested.

But she had promised to read it. Lionel had, anyway.

"Dear Amanda," she read, her heels tapping against the limestone.

I hope that you had a safe journey back home. I also hope that you are not repulsed by this letter. I do not mean to cause you any discomfort. I simply wish to keep in touch. I did take the liberty of asking your friend, June, whether she thought it would be appropriate for me to send a letter and, I must say, she encouraged me with wild fervor. I must also hope that, having given such enthusiastic advice, she won't now be placed on your blacklist. June is a wonderful friend and deserves the best, don't you agree?

Well, that was quite thoughtful of him, to worry about June like that, Amanda thought. She'd say it again: David and June had potential. She really must encourage that angle.

She told me that you left for home unexpectedly, at

*your parents' urgent request. Though I am sure they are
delighted to have you back in their company, I must say
that I am feeling intensely sorry for myself. I had looked
forward to the chance for us to get to know each other
better during the week of Fiesta. You may not have realized it at the time, but my heart was in grave danger of
fluttering out of my chest each time I happened to
catch your eye during our day together near Puyé. (I
don't know what gives me the courage to write that.)*

"Oh my, he is a romantic, isn't he?" Amanda said out
loud. She rolled her eyes.

*Although the day was spoiled by my ridiculous lack of
concentration, which managed to wedge the car so
firmly in the mud, I must admit that I had hopes of
making it up to you this week with some less fraught
activity: loop-de-loops in an aeroplane, perhaps, or
learning to tightrope across canyons. Haha. Well, all
right, I actually was thinking about dancing with you at
the Fiesta's Spanish baile. But I better be careful about
even writing about that. I had been musing on just that
very thing when I drove us into the mud hole. Clearly,
the image transports me from this world. If I'm not careful, I'll look to see my lap covered in ink.*
   Oh dear.
   Back again, having cleaned up.

Amanda laughed, in spite of herself. She had to admit
he wrote a good letter.

Truly, I want you to know that I will be imagining your

face behind every mask at the ball tonight. (Please don't be concerned. I have taken the precaution of placing the inkpot some distance away.) Although my mind knows that you will not be near, my heart is happiest when it hopes.

Finally . . . and most seriously . . . I want to mention how much I admire the quest that you have set for yourself. I have much sympathy for your view, often feeling that way myself. Feet on the ground, with a mind open to the world? I have some small hope that someday I may count myself among the lucky ones who have found such a place in the world. And surely, it must be the fact that I am writing—instead of conversing at a dance—that makes me bold enough to say so, but I have always hoped to find a girl who can see herself as clearly, well beyond the conventions. Indeed, I have some wild hope that I have found her . . . though she bravely pursues this quest several thousand miles away.

Can I hope that you will take pity on me and respond? I trust I have not put you off by my serious tone. Please ignore it, if you would rather. In fact, if you will even consider sending a reply, I would be happy to obey any directive you may have. Indeed, if necessary, I would be more than willing to restrict my words to ruminations on the weather.

Yours in cloudy conditions with hope for clear skies,
David

Holding tightly to the letter, Amanda drew up her knees and gazed toward Santa Fe and the plateaus beyond. The sun was close to setting—it must be nearly seven o'clock, she'd better head back soon—and the clouds that had moved into the sky over the afternoon were now tinged with pink. She was stunned, not by the landscape but by David's letter. Frankly, she had expected something whiny. Or maybe just superficial. Instead she found herself marveling at his insight. After all, he approved of her quest, didn't he?

Whatever was she going to say?

Could he really hope to find a girl who saw herself clearly, well beyond the conventions? Was it possible that he not only understood what she was doing but liked her for it? But wait, didn't she describe the ideal woman that way, at Hal's party, when they were discussing girls? He hadn't been very supportive then—just laughed. Was he just being one of the boys? Her ebullience abruptly switched to paranoia. Had David seen through her disguise? Was he writing in code, to let her know? She felt kind of sick, worried she'd been taken for a fool. Honestly, when she thought about it, who would say yes to having a total stranger read a love letter? Yet she could have sworn that his sentiments yesterday had been genuine. How would she ever know for sure? She probably missed something in his tone, especially since she'd been steaming mad at Hal.

Hal. No uncertainty there. The scheme to make him jealous was a jewel.

Stick to the plan, she admonished herself. Forget about David and his letter. And keep to her path. The letter was probably just a prank. She stuffed it into her pocket. Besides, she needed every bit of her brain right now to work out how to charm Bob Hunt.

But, for a second, she let herself wonder. Would David really try to imagine her face behind every mask tonight?

SIX

Lionel was standing next to the Santa Fe Armory, watching for June and the others. Despite the late hour, whole families were arriving. Lionel had been caught in a brief rain shower on his way back from the mountain, but now constellations littered the sky. Inside, the armory was brightly lit and, from what Lionel could see through the building's high windows, the walls and ceiling were festooned with crepe paper strings in vivid primary colors. Joyful fiddling had already begun. Boys and girls, standing in line with their parents and amazed to be up so late, skipped to the strains of music escaping through the entrance, tiny lace veils swinging across the girls' shoulders as they twirled.

The gay music didn't soothe Lionel, who was anxious on two counts. First, he worried that David had uncovered the disguise and would not only make fun of Lionel but, more important, ruin the opportunity to put the Bob Hunt plan into action. Second, on top of being nervous about whether he could lure Bob Hunt away, now he wondered if he'd even be able to recognize him. Everyone, babies to grandparents, was in costume. Lionel himself was now doubly disguised. The matador costume was outrageously fancy: tight purple satin trousers were decorated with a strip of metallic embroidery, and the same glitzy embroidery blanketed the jacket, with shoulder caps so stiff they felt like steel. A purple cape lined in red covered his back. The jacket sleeves were a little long and the hat too big—it kept falling into his eyes—but at least he fit in.

He heard June's laugh—a pleasant trill that rang out above the festive music and crowd murmurs—before he saw her, walking arm and arm with David and Justin, both dressed as vaqueros. They all wore masks. David's trousers—three-quarter length and wide—were a cautious brown, but Justin had chosen bright green with a yellow stripe running along the bottom hem. A yellow-and-green-striped bandana hung around his neck. Both boys sported wide-brimmed black hats, tall riding boots, and green and red serapes.

June outshone everyone. Just look at her, Lionel thought, taking in the transformation. How could Justin resist? Irrepressibly cheerful, June usually brought to mind the midwestern girl her mother had been, an apple-cheeked innocent with tastes that tended toward demure dresses decked with buttons and bows. But tonight June had imported a little fire. Always graceful, she strode along as if in front of an audience of thousands. A black blouse, tailored to her figure, was tucked into a ruffled skirt that dipped down to her calves. And what a skirt! Black ruffles over pink, on the right; pink ruffles over black, on the left. A shawl spilling huge gardenias in brilliant shades of red, pink, orange, and yellow was knotted at her waist.

Spotting Lionel, June instinctively dropped the arms of David and Justin to hold out her hands for an enthusiastic embrace that, too late, she remembered was meant for Amanda, not Lionel. "I'm so glad you came," June said, awkwardly grasping Lionel's shoulders. "Oops!" she whispered, before stepping back, laughing. Looking over her shoulder at the boys, she said, "Oh dear, Lionel, I hope you'll excuse me. Fiesta infects me like this sometimes. Makes everyone seem like family."

"I thought it might be the sight of a matador that inspired such admiration," Lionel said, nodding toward David and Justin. "Don't we all look dapper?"

"Christopher's?" Justin asked, taking in Lionel's costume.

"He wore it year before last, I think," June answered. "It looks good on you," she said to Lionel. "You know, my brother, Jim, is here tonight, and he's brought his Brownie. He said he'd take a photo of all of us later. You'll join us, won't you? We could mail you a copy."

"I'd be happy to," Lionel said, striking a pose. "My life as a matador."

David laughed, but raised his eyebrows slightly while reaching out to shake Lionel's hand. "Talk later?" he said quietly. "Letter?"

Lionel nodded, his heart sinking. How long could he dare put him off? It should have been a simple matter—tell him to send the darn letter—but now mistrust of his motives made Lionel wary. Perhaps he'd lose him in the crowded armory, where dancers already covered the floor in a brisk two-step. Along the edges, small giggling girls in threes and fours held hands and swung in circles. The baile was cherished by every family whose Spanish roots went deep—and there were plenty—because it honored traditions reaching back through Mexico's reign all the way to

Spain. But everyone in Santa Fe was invited to the baile, one of the town's biggest social events.

At the back of the room, volunteers—middle-aged women, mostly—kept the punch bowls full and the cookie plates stacked with biscochitos. Seated along the west wall, elderly women in black dresses, with lace veils flowing from ornate mantillas, cautioned spinning children or gazed fondly at a dancing couple. Older men—husbands and fathers—in starched white shirts under short black jackets—congregated in the corners of the room, smoking cigars and exchanging dire weather forecasts for the upcoming winter.

"There you are!" cried Teresa, emerging from the cluster of her family gathered next to her grandmother, one of the reigning matrons. Teresa's cheeks were flushed, and her brown eyes were lit with sparks of gold. Her dark shimmering hair, the deep black of an unlit cave, glinted with highlights of blue under the lights. Like June, Teresa was dressed as Spanish nobility, but her dress of plum brocade had once been her grandmother's. A fringed green shawl embellished with lilac-colored embroidery hung from her arms, showing off bare shoulders. "It's so crowded! I think everyone in town is here."

"Including us, now!" June said laughing. "You look marvelous, Teresa."

"Smashing!" Justin said. He pointed to her dance card, tied at her wrist. "I'm here to claim my dance," he said. "Next one?"

"You're just in time," Teresa said. "I'm dying to dance. I was just about to threaten my brothers." Behind her, two of her older brothers laughed, extending their hands toward Justin, David, and Lionel, but the third kept his arms crossed against his chest, glowering. He was the tallest of the three and built like a ponderosa pine.

"You won't begrudge Teresa this dance, will you?" Justin asked Gilberto, who seemed to have put himself in charge of Teresa. "I promised Christopher, you know." Gilberto nodded but kept his eyes on the couple as Justin signed Teresa's dance card and led her toward the dance floor.

June, in some despair, caught Lionel's eye before smiling at David. "Help me with this?" June said to David, pointing to her own dance card.

"Happy to," said David.

"They're silly, really, these dance cards," June explained to Lionel, while David fastened the card's string around June's wrist. "Like we're back in the 1880s. We all diligently fill in a name or two and then forget all about them. But parents think they're essential. And it's kind of fun." She shook it, watching it sway at the end of her arm. "Especially if it contains the signatures of men of extraordinary charm," she said pointedly.

David laughed. "Surely you don't mean me, June," he said. "But I'd be honored to have that dance, if I may." He scribbled his name on her card. "I think I remember how," he said, throwing a slightly panicked look at Lionel before he and June disappeared into the crowd of dancers.

Lionel watched for a moment as Justin and Teresa swung into view. Clearly at his most charming, Justin was whispering a story into Teresa's ear, bringing a smile and brightening her already vivid eyes. Lionel decided he could leave Gilberto in charge of Justin while he searched for Hal. Touring the room, he passed June's brother, Jim, dressed in baggy pants and stationed near the punch bowl. He had just turned thirteen and, Lionel knew through talks with him at June's, so far new-fangled inventions beat out girls for his attention. His pride, the latest Brownie Hawkeye camera, was slung around his neck. Lionel caught himself just before he said hello. As Lionel, he and Jim would never have met. June's parents were dancing nearby, talking animatedly, occasionally calling out to friends. On the surface, they didn't appear to be worried about Amanda's sudden disappearance, but Lionel felt guilty all the same and ducked into a crowd. June and David were starting another dance, a waltz this time, and June looked not only ravishing, but extremely happy. What could they be talking about with such enthusiasm? Was it Lionel's secret? You're being ridiculous, he told himself. But next thing he knew, he was tapping David on the shoulder.

"Cut in?" he asked, holding out his arms to June while avoiding David's eyes.

"How nice!" June said. "You don't mind, do you, David?" As soon as he had stepped away, she whispered to Lionel, "I couldn't believe how dumb I was about the hug! But I don't think anyone noticed. David didn't say anything, anyway." Lionel let out a breath. Maybe all was well after all. Now he felt silly for worrying. Well, at least his impulsive behavior would give him a few minutes to talk with June, who might be able to point out Hal. "Still, we'd better behave with complete decorum while we're dancing, just in case. By the way, you lead very well," June teased.

"The price of being tall," Lionel said. "Always had to take the boy's part at dance lessons. Though it is paying off handsomely. So how is it going with you and David?" Lionel questioned. "Did he agree to help?"

"Well," June said, "he doesn't actually know about the

plan yet. I meant to tell him, but then he went on and on about you . . . Amanda, I mean, not Lionel . . . and with such passion, I might say . . . that we never quite got around to it. Honestly, in all the years I've known him, I don't think I've ever heard him talk so much. But it won't matter. We've been friends so long, he won't think twice about my putting myself in his way. All he's really thinking about right now is you—you, Amanda—and that letter. So, what do you think?"

"Mmm, interesting. He seems to have a very good sense of humor."

"He does," June said firmly, still eager to interest Amanda in David. When she'd written to David, she knew nothing about Amanda's resolution to shun romance. After he arrived, she was sorry she had asked him, worried that David would be bored by Amanda's monologues about finding herself. Certainly, everyone else was. Too late, she saw that it was Amanda who seemed unmoved. David was head over heels. Poor him. It made June feel bad and she was still trying to think of how to encourage a second look. "So, good interesting?"

"Just interesting." Lionel really didn't want to talk about it. "I'm going to tell him to send the letter. It's easier than trying to talk him out of it. I'll write what I really think when I get home."

June sighed with disappointment. "Well, let him down gently, all right? He's a good friend."

"Promise," Lionel said, cursing himself when he realized he had inadvertently steered them close to Justin and Teresa, who waved.

"Ouch," June said, waving weakly back.

"Sorry!" Lionel said to June. "At least Gilberto's on

76

watch. I am planning to talk with Justin later. Thought I'd check whether he's noticed you and David. And, you know, it wouldn't hurt for you to chat with Teresa. If it's not too awkward?" As the dance ended, they stood a moment together, jostled by a crowd of cowgirls, peasants, and Spanish aristocrats.

"I'm sort of afraid to find out," June said.

"Could be good news, you know," Lionel said, holding June's elbow and trying to maneuver them both through the crowd. A huge clown blocked their path. "It's hard to believe these are your neighbors!" Lionel laughed. "Which reminds me, do you know if Mr. Bynner is here?"

"I'm sure he is, let me look." June gave up trying to move forward and instead glanced around the hall. "Over there!" she exclaimed, gesturing toward the entrance. Lionel watched as Bynner, in a purple Navajo shirt, cupped his hand around his mouth to talk into the ear of a friend whose head was covered by a monk's hood.

Lionel came to attention, like a hit man spotting his prey.

"So, did you enjoy yourself at June's party?" Teresa asked Justin, as they began the waltz. "I wanted to go, but at the last minute my parents said we were going to visit my great-aunt. She's housebound and wanted to see everyone's costumes."

"June's?" Justin answered, looking at Teresa in some confusion. The festivities made her radiant, and his arms tightened around her. He had forgotten everything up to this moment, even Gilberto's watchful stare. He hadn't felt this crazy about a girl since, well, ever. If he played his cards right, he was sure he could talk Teresa into letting him walk her home. There were plenty of dark corners between here and there for kisses. Just look at those eyes. She had to be thinking about him, right? Not Christopher? He really thought she was the one, not just forbidden fruit, like he'd been telling the guys. This time would be different. Although he did feel a little guilty about Christopher. But Christopher knew him and his ways, right? And asked Justin to take care of Teresa anyway? It was almost like Christopher was inviting him to fall in love. Wasn't it? It was easy to imagine the touch of her lips, and he knew all the sheltered entryways around the Plaza. They'd have to ditch Gilberto, though. If he could be distracted, Justin might try talking Teresa into stepping outside right now. He wrenched his eyes away from hers to scan the room.

On the lookout for Gilberto, Justin was startled instead to see Lionel cutting in on David and June, whose face lit up as she moved into Lionel's arms. He couldn't remember ever seeing June give such a warm welcome to a boy. Except himself, of course. But they were old friends. Why would she be so eager to dance with Lionel? She couldn't be falling for him, could she? Justin thought Lionel was kind of strange. All that yammering on about girls knowing themselves. Justin didn't think someone like that would be June's cup of tea at all. Yet there they were, chattering away as if they'd known each other all their lives.

He had the feeling something was going on, but he didn't know what. It had been in the back of his mind, ever since meeting June and Lionel at Kaune's. She had been acting kind of secretive. Was Lionel involved somehow? But, even if he was, why did June need to keep it a secret? Especially from Justin?

"The party tonight? June's house?" Teresa said, looking at Justin warily. "Friendly get-together?"

"What do you think of Lionel?" Justin asked abruptly. "Nice guy? A little too smooth?"

"Lionel?" She followed Justin's gaze. "Seems nice enough," Teresa said. "But I only met him at lunch, remember? June and he seem to be getting along well." Teresa glanced again at the couple, whose dancing had brought them near. Teresa waved at June. "Was he at June's party?"

"No, not at the party," Justin said. "Though I did run into them this morning coming out of Kaune's."

"Wouldn't it be wonderful if they like each other?" Teresa said enthusiastically. "She deserves the best, don't you think?"

"Of course I do," Justin answered. "Absolutely. I just wonder if Lionel *is* the best."

"Well, I don't know why you're asking me. You took him to Mr. Bynner's party, didn't you? What did you think?"

"Nice enough," Justin said. "A regular guy. But I wanted a girl's opinion. June's like a sister, you know. Maybe I just feel overprotective."

"Like you protect me?" Teresa teased. With the dance ending, they made their way through the crush toward David and the refreshments.

"Ab-so-lute-ly," Justin said as Gilberto sauntered over. He'd forgotten all about distracting him. No opportunity now. "I wonder, would you mind talking with June?" he said, placing a glass of punch in Teresa's hand. "See what she has to say about Lionel. I need to talk with David about something. When we dance again—you'll dance with me again, won't you?—you can tell me what you found out."

"Hey, you two," David said. "What a mob, eh? Jim said

he'd take our photo, if we can round up everyone. Guess June is with Lionel?" He glanced at the crowd, catching sight of the bobbing matador's hat blocked by a huge clown.

"So would you excuse us, Teresa?" Justin asked, seizing David's shoulder and pushing him toward the door. "We'll be right back." Teresa wouldn't think twice about him leaving her. She'd guess he just wanted a swig.

"Hey!" David said. "What are you doing?"

"Fresh air," Justin answered. Outside, fiesta revelers stood in groups, heads together, deep in conversation. Others huddled against the armory's wall, discreetly passing a bottle. Justin dragged David partway down Washington Street toward the Plaza.

"Want a sip?" David asked, when they had settled on the small wall surrounding the square. He pulled a flask from underneath the serape. The night's crisp air raised goosebumps along his arm after the armory's teeming warmth. "Is that what this is about?" He took a quick swig, then passed the flask to Justin. "Or, I bet I know why you dragged me out here. You're looking for romantic advice. About Teresa." He shook his head at Justin. "I saw the way you looked at her while dancing. You need to be careful. That's my advice. And Gilberto's."

"No, no, not that. It's all under control, no need to worry," Justin said, folding his arms under the serape, still holding on to the flask. He looked at David intently. "No, I have a question. About Lionel. I saw him cut in while you were dancing, and I'm curious. Do you think they've met before?"

"Who?"

"June and Lionel."

David looked incredulous. "Why would you even think that?"

Justin paused, surprised by his own vehemence. Tonight was his and Teresa's. What did he care? Lionel would be on a train in a day or two. Besides, June was hardly Miss Mystery. No one was more aboveboard. Then he remembered her warm smile as Lionel had cut in. Maybe it wasn't his business, but damned if he was going to be left in the dark. "I ran into them this morning, coming out of Kaune's. June seemed kind of embarrassed about being seen with him. And then, when she mentioned the get-together tonight, they seemed almost to be speaking in code. Like she was warning Lionel against coming to the house. Or something." When David looked doubtful, Justin continued. "And when I asked June if she wanted to walk with me to the Plaza, she said no. Couldn't get away from me fast enough. Like she had something to hide."

David scratched his head. "Secret code? Something to hide? That's not our June."

"Do you think it could be a secret engagement or something?" Justin asked. The idea hit him suddenly, an arrow into his heart. "What if they met months ago and have been in a secret correspondence? Then they arranged for him to show up 'by accident.'"

"You've read too many novels. And why do you care, anyway?"

"Just the mystery," Justin protested. "The secretiveness. It's fishy. I don't want to stand by if she's been taken in by some charlatan."

"I'll pay attention, but I haven't noticed anything. And, well, frankly, I kind of have the impression that June has suddenly become interested in me. Romantically, I mean.

Tonight, at her house, she seemed to be everywhere I turned." David half-smiled, remembering June squeezing onto the porch swing with him. "Not that I'm complaining," David said. "She's a lovely girl. But it's crazy. I've been pouring my heart out to her. She knows I'm nuts about Amanda." David threw open his hands, bewildered. "Girls."

"She seemed pleased about Lionel cutting in, though?"

"Didn't strike me one way or another. Besides, June's one of the most open and friendly girls I know. I just think she's trying to make him feel welcome. He really doesn't know anyone in town."

"Except the professor and his wife."

"Huh?"

"He couldn't come to June's because he was having dinner with a professor and his wife. He met them traveling."

"Well, all right. Two others besides us."

"Justin! David!" Jim was striding toward them. "Come back inside. I'm trying to get everyone together for a picture."

"All right," Justin said. He handed the flask back to David. "Anyway, if you notice anything suspicious, tell me. All right?"

"Fine," said David. "But I think you're barking up the wrong tree."

"Maybe," Justin said, unconvinced. "Hey, thanks for the drink."

"Tell Jim I'll be there in a minute."

Bracing his hands on the wall and tipping his head back, David gazed at the stars that lit the sky. He didn't feel quite ready to join the others while feeling so hopeless. Wasn't there a song about constellations shining down on distant lovers? Not that he and Amanda were lovers. Hardly even acquaintances. He sighed, frustration binding every muscle into tiny knots. This could have been such an amazing night. He and Amanda would have danced, surely? If only to be polite. Given that chance, he would have showed her how much he cared. He would have tried to say everything he had written in that letter. The thought of the letter made his heart sink. He'd been so hopeful. With every pen swipe, he had imagined her reading, understanding, wishing. Now, because Lionel hadn't told him straight out what he thought, he just felt stupid. The situation felt messy and out of control. He should never have written the damn thing. He especially should never have let Lionel read it.

He absently watched the costumed partygoers milling around the armory entrance. A woman walked sideways through the door to accommodate her sixteenth-century gown, while a matador and monk slipped behind her. With a start, David recognized the garishly purple costumed bullfighter as Lionel, but the monk? Maybe the professor Justin had mentioned. They were strolling down the opposite side of the street, deep in conversation. Neither noticed David. Halfway down the block, the monk threw back his hood, and David let out a snort. He guessed that Justin could chuck his concerns. That was Bob Hunt, Hal's friend. If he and Lionel were out for a walk, David figured he knew why. Everyone suspected that he and Hal were of the same persuasion. Though it did strike him funny that Lionel had appeared so alarmed yesterday when told about Hal's party. Probably just playacting so he wouldn't be found out. At any rate, Justin should have no worries about June. Lionel might be involved in a hidden romance, but not with her.

"Where did everyone go?" June asked Teresa, who was standing near the punch with a glass in her hand. "Jim said he would take our photo, but now I don't see him anywhere. Do you?"

"He was just here," Teresa said, standing on her toes to look over the crowd. She spotted Lionel heading toward Hal and his friends. "David and Justin went outside a minute ago. To 'talk.' As if I'm not supposed to know what that means."

"Hopefully they'll be back by the time I locate Jim."

"And Lionel's over in the corner with Hal and his friends," Teresa said. "I saw you dancing with Lionel. You looked awfully happy," she said, stretching out the last word.

June laughed, suddenly confused. Whatever she told Teresa was bound to find its way to Justin's ears, for better or worse. She'd better choose her words carefully. "He's so interesting, Teresa. Imagine, planning to go to Hollywood as a writer. It's just one story after another with him. Fascinating."

"So you like him?"

"Of course, I like him, Teresa. But, oh, not that way. Besides, he'll be on the train to California in a day or two. So there really isn't much of a chance for us, even if I wanted."

"Oh really," Teresa said, and June blushed. "Anyway, Justin and I were glad to see you looking so happy. You deserve it, June."

At Justin's name, June came to attention. "You, too, Teresa. I bet you can't wait to see Christopher again."

"Oh, June! If you only knew." Knew what? thought June,

panicked. "I am so impatient to see Christopher. Christopher. I love saying his name, you know? That's the most wonderful thing about being in love. The thrill each time you get to say his name, like it's your own. My own Christopher."

Oh, thank god, June thought, relief washing over her like a summer monsoon. Lionel was right. Maybe this could turn out well.

"In Christopher's last letter, he said he would likely be here for Christmas," Teresa said. "Maybe next summer, he'll be back for good, if he gets a place at Vigil and Johnson. Then we can be engaged. Truly engaged." Her tone held such longing.

"Oh, I hope so, Teresa! We'd be sisters then forever." She hugged her. "And Justin, Teresa?" June asked, the conversation's turn giving her courage. "I've seen the way he looks at you."

"Oh, June. You know him better than anyone, don't you? I know you've always liked him, but really, I'm not sure he could ever be serious with anyone. It's just a game with him. That's why I was so happy to see you and Lionel together." Teresa stood on tiptoes again, looking toward the corner, but Lionel was no longer part of Hal's circle.

"I told you, there's nothing like that going on," June said, more sharply than she intended. She'd better nip this story in the bud, or she'd just end up spilling the beans. "Lionel's a fascinating guy, Teresa. And maybe you're right about Justin." It broke her heart to hear herself say it. But no time to switch courses now. "Now David. . . ." June stopped and looked at Teresa meaningfully.

"David! Really? Oh, June, I always thought you and he would be wonderful together." Teresa began to paint a glowing picture of life happily ever after for June and David, but a minute or two of such talk was all June could stand. She couldn't bear to think what that lie might cost in the long run, for David, if not for her.

"Teresa, it looks like we've lost everyone now! I'm going to look for Jim. Let's set a time for the photo, all right? That's a good plan, don't you think?"

"Sure. Though, here's Jim now, with Justin behind." At Justin's name, June's heart stopped. Teresa was right. A loved one's name *was* the most beautiful thing in the world.

"But no David. Or Lionel either, now." In the corner, Hal and his friends were nearly doubled over with laughter, but there was no sign of Lionel. "Jim," June called out, waving him over. "Can we set a time for the photo? Around midnight? It seems like we just get one person when we lose another."

"Who's missing?" Jim asked. "David's outside, he said he'd be here in a minute."

"Oh, I guess nearly everyone is here then," June said doubtfully. "But Lionel's not. And I told him he could be in the picture." She became aware of Justin's sudden attention. Did she just say something dumb, like calling Lionel Amanda? She glanced around, but no one else seemed disturbed. This is why I never lie, she thought. I'll only get caught. Better to dance, where she could safely keep her mouth shut. Spotting David entering the armory, she walked toward him, calling to the others, "Midnight! Here!" She pointed at the photographer's corner, then laughed as she pulled David onto the dance floor.

Around midnight, the entire group was assembling. Jim was urging June and Teresa to stand closer. Black curtains hung behind them, tacked to the wall, in the area set aside for photographs. Lionel, standing behind Teresa and June, thoughtfully stroked his mustache and tried to stand steady. He was practically tipsy with success, helped along by a half flask of rotgut. Lord, the things he had to do to defend Mabel. But the plan could not have played out better. The first thing he saw, as he and Bob stepped back into the armory, was Hal with eyes on the door, as if he'd been scanning the area every second. At their entrance, a sliver of pain had pierced those eyes before feigning nonchalance. All according to script, as far as Lionel was concerned. First, Mabel's torment, now Hal's anguish. A tooth for a tooth.

"The hired photographer will be back from his break soon," Jim told everyone as David and Justin walked up. Jim pointed to their places behind the girls, then urged them all to stand even closer. Trying to follow Jim's orders, Lionel stumbled and David's hand on his back, meant to steady him, quickened his heart instead, like a flash of lightning. Blame it on the liquor?

"Thanks, old man," Lionel said, receiving David's quick nod.

"He's letting me use his flash," Jim said. "It's the absolute latest! So, now, everyone smile . . . say 'green chile'! Then we'll do one more." Everyone in the group sang out, "green chile!" then waited for the second shot. David called out, "When you finish, Jim, I'll take one of you and the girls."

"All right," Jim said, "But now, on the count of three, everyone . . . 'green chile'!"

When Jim handed David the camera after the shot and

stood next to the girls, Justin and Lionel stepped to the side to watch.

"So what do you think of our little dance?" Justin asked. "Does it measure up?"

"Ab-so-lute-ly," Lionel said. "Lucky I happened to be in Santa Fe for Fiesta, isn't it? I couldn't have timed it better."

"Yes, very lucky," Justin said, glancing at David, who simply closed his eyes and shook his head, before focusing the camera. The photo took just a second, then June and Teresa walked over to the boys, while Jim took care of the equipment.

"That was so thoughtful of you, David," June said. "My parents will be so pleased."

"Happy to do it."

"You know, David," June said, hooking her arm through his, while including the others in her glance. "We really should offer to take Lionel to Indian Fair tomorrow. Remember we talked about it at La Fonda?" Justin, who was just about to ask Teresa for a dance, hung back.

"That's right," David said, clearly flustered by June's continuing attention. "You were hoping to see Indian art, weren't you, Lionel? Pottery? Paintings?"

"I was," Lionel said. "Is Indian Fair here? Or do we have to travel?"

"Right here. Just around the corner, anyway," June said, before looking fully into David's eyes. "David, can we make a date to meet Lionel and take him to Indian Fair?"

"Of course," David said. "Noon?"

"Oh, a little later, please," Lionel said. "I need at least a few hours sleep. Two o'clock?"

"Perfect," June said. "We'll stop by the hotel." She glanced at Justin, as if about to include him in the invitation as well, then stopped. "David," she said instead, "another dance?"

❖

In the back of the ballroom, a group of children were taking turns charging like a bull, while Lionel waved his cape at them. When he whipped it away, the children broke into peals of laughter, which Lionel suspected was as much due to the late hour as to the silliness of the game. They should stop soon, before laughter turned to tears.

"Lionel!" David called out, approaching. Lionel folded the cape over his arm and held out a warning hand to the next child getting ready to charge. He waved at David, trying furiously to come up with an excuse. If only he had ducked out a minute ago. "Do you have time to talk?" David said, as he moved closer.

"Sure," Lionel said. "Just give me a minute. I have a few more bulls to fight." He pointed to the child next in line and then two other children, who were pretending to paw with their feet. "Three more. Then I have to go." When the third child had charged, the rest began to whine, but Lionel fixed them with a look. "I could use some fresh air," Lionel said to David. "How about you?"

The temperature past midnight was rapidly dropping into the fifties. Walking outside was like dipping into a cold pool after a long soak in a hot spring. "How did you get roped into playing with the kids?" David asked.

"I don't even know," Lionel answered. The gaiety from his drink with Bob had worn off, leaving him with a sour stomach and a pounding head. He still experienced a twinge of satisfaction from the ploy though. "I was just kind of standing there, and one of the smallest children decided to charge at me. I took off my cape to play, and the next thing I knew I was surrounded by pint-sized people."

"Well, sorry to drag you away, but I was hoping to talk."

"Oh, you saved me, believe me," Lionel said. "I meant to find you earlier, but I wasn't sure about disturbing you. You and June make a nice couple." One lie, one half lie.

David groaned. "I like June. Always have. But as a friend, you know? I don't know what's got into her. I'm flattered but very confused. I don't want to hurt her feelings. And she knows how I feel about Amanda."

"She's probably just trying to make you feel better," Lionel said.

He gave a big sigh of relief. "Oh, I'm glad you see it that way, too. I guess I should just have asked her. I'm all mixed up." He smiled sheepishly, then drew a deep breath. "Anyway, you know how I feel about Amanda. Well, you should anyway. Can I ask? What did you think? Was it horrible?"

Lionel made his hand into a fist and socked him on the shoulder. "Not at all." Then he looked at David doubtfully. "Well, all right, it did take me by surprise. I'm not sure I could have been that honest." He pulled the letter from inside his jacket. "Here you go," he said.

"It's trash, isn't it?" David said, sorrowfully, pocketing the letter. "I'm a dope. Thank god I didn't send it. Now I'm just embarrassed that you saw it."

"No, no, I didn't mean that," Lionel said. What did he mean? He had had all night to think of what to say to David, but hadn't come up with a thing. He was pretty sure, as a guy, that he was supposed to warn David against sending a letter like that. But, well, it actually was the right sort of letter to send Amanda. If she had a heart available. Which she didn't, Lionel reminded himself firmly. Anyway, how could he say something thing like that without sounding like a girl? Should he take David into his confidence and come clean? But facing him as Amanda sounded terrifying. It was easier to be Lionel.

"It's not trash. I admired it," Lionel said. "You have a way with words. And you're funny. Girls like that," he said, which made David's shoulders relax. "But tell me," Lionel said, buying time. "What do you think Amanda thought of you?"

"Honestly? She barely offered a glance. Looked right through me. But June told me later I shouldn't take it personally. Amanda just isn't interested in anyone right now, I guess. Had a bad breakup or something. But even if there'd been any interest, it would have drowned when I drove into that quagmire . . . Lord!" he said, looking down at his feet.

"She made fun of you?" Lionel asked, thinking that he ought to at least try to set the record straight while he had the opportunity. "Or was annoyed or something?"

"No," David said, thinking back to the drive home from the picnic. "Not really. In fact, she was about as cheerful and helpful as she could be. Though she didn't pay me any special attention. No attention at all. It made me feel invisible. I just felt like a dolt. God, I'm ridiculous. You'd have kept your wits about you, Lionel."

"Oh, I don't know," he said. "Anyway, I doubt she saw it that way. Seems to me you're being kind of hard on yourself."

"Maybe," David said doubtfully. "But that's why I wanted to send the letter. Start again. You think maybe it's okay? I hoped she'd be intrigued. Though maybe I'm crazy even to think she'd care." His fears kept open the pit of worry in his stomach.

"I guess I'd say you hit the right tone." Lionel thought back to the part of the letter where David had mentioned Amanda's feet on the ground, but a mind open to the world. "And this quest?" Lionel asked.

David's eyes grew dreamy in the lamplight. "You know,

she's just different from most of the girls I know. Even girls who think they're modern. She isn't like that at all. To me, she seemed focused. Not on unimportant things. Society things. Girl things. She seemed like she was trying to create a life. You know? That's why I was so disappointed that I didn't get to know her better. Or, maybe, that she didn't get a chance to know me better. Know that I'm interested in being with a girl who likes looking at the world, trying to find her way. Interested in the old ways. Interested in how the land here affects you." He studied the parts of the Plaza that could be seen in pools of lamplight. "I know she liked it here. You may not have had a chance to take it in, but I've lived here awhile now. The land brings clarity. Makes you feel like you're a part of something bigger. I've felt that way for as long as I've been looking at it. But I'd never heard a girl talk about it." He laughed. "Well, all right, she could go on and on about it, like she was the first ever to discover it. But it was still a pleasure to listen."

"Is that so?" Lionel said, disconcerted suddenly by the criticism amid glowing praise. He was ready to revert to his paranoia—could David's feelings be real?—when his attention turned toward the cathedral, towering at the end of the street. He imagined being Amanda again, back home, with no letter on its way. It made Lionel miss David, even though he was inches away. "You know what I say? Send it. She may be intrigued. And what if she isn't? The worst that can happen is that she won't respond. Well, it's not like you'll run into her around here, right? It's the best thing about a letter, don't you think?"

"Yeah," said David, his voice still dazed and dreamy. "Though, right at the moment? I'd love to see her face-to-face."

"Then I say send it. Maybe you'll get your chance."

"I will," David said. "Send the letter, I mean. And, Lionel, thanks. You've been a huge help. Not only offering to read the letter, but listening to me ramble. I don't mind telling you, I was so worried. I thought you were avoiding me because the letter was a disaster. A lot of guys would have said flat out, chuck it and forget her. There's no way they would have heard me out. Makes me feel like we're old friends."

"Happy to help." Lionel said, reaching out his hand to shake. Behind them, lights flickered in the armory and crowds of people began to pour out of the door. When David took his hand, Lionel latched on, feeling that same electric surge as during the photograph. Could it still be the liquor? Forgetting, his fingers tightened in David's hand. When he saw David's eyes grow slightly alarmed, Lionel dropped his hand to his side as quickly as he could.

"Gosh, I'm about ready to drop," Lionel stammered. He didn't know which shocked him more. Feeling the surge, or forgetting his part in this pageant. "Hardly know what I'm doing. Listen," he rushed, "tell the others thanks so much for a wonderful evening, but I think I better go back to the hotel, all right? I look forward to seeing you and June tomorrow, though. At two." He turned his back on the crowds coming out of the armory and hurried off toward La Fonda, with David watching, mouth agape.

SEVEN

"There you are, David!" June stepped out of the crowd of costumed merrymakers that was surging past. Behind them, near the armory door, Justin stood talking with Teresa and her brothers. "Another perfect Grand Baile, don't you think?"

"It was fun," David admitted. He shoved away the alarming fact of Lionel's tender handshake. Anyway, it didn't matter now. David gripped Amanda's letter beneath his serape, his fingers gently caressing it as if he had hold of Amanda's palm. Happiness welled at the thought of sending the envelope on its journey, straight into her hands.

"By the way, have you seen Lionel?" June asked. "I wanted to say good night."

"He just left," David said. "Said he was sorry to leave so abruptly, but it had been a long night. Frankly, he did look a little worse for the wear."

"Oh dear. I hope he had a good time." June glanced back at Justin, still talking with Gilberto and Teresa. "Walk me home, David?" June asked. "I want to ask you something."

"Of course," David answered, but he was taken aback. June wasn't planning to suddenly bare her feelings for him, was she? He shoved the letter into his pants pocket. He'd post it on his way home. "You don't want to wait for Justin?"

"Well, actually . . ." June said, pulling him aside and finally letting him in on the plan—they were supposed to act like they were in love to make Justin jealous. A silly, foolish scheme, David thought. And so out of character for June. On the other hand, knowing Justin, it would probably work. He sighed and offered her his arm.

Twenty minutes later, having seen June safely to her house, David walked to the post office across from the cathedral. He opened the mail slot, drew a deep breath, and then dropped in the letter, listening to its whisper as it floated onto a stack of other mail. No turning back now. He smiled. His words, seen and blessed by Lionel, were on their way.

Although nearly three in the morning, couples held hands and strolled along the middle of the street. A Spanish duke and his lady stopped to kiss by the bridge. As David passed the cathedral and then headed toward Canyon Road on his way to his mother's house, he began humming a song he'd heard recently. He was self-conscious about his voice—could barely hold a tune—but the lyrics matched his emotions so well that he couldn't hold back. Voice cracking, he sang softly, "If I could be with you, one hour tonight, if I was free to do the things that I might, I'm tellin' ya true, I'd be anythin' but blue, if I could be with you . . ."

Someday . . . if all went well, if the stars aligned, if his luck changed . . . he and Amanda would be together, like the duke and his lady who hugged each other close as they ambled down the road. David would pull Amanda near, kissing her forehead, murmuring sweet nothings. She'd squeeze his hand, snuggle beneath his shoulder. They'd share their dreams. They'd make their plans.

Though first, of course, the letter had to reach her. He envisioned her opening it, reading it, feeling for him what he felt for her—that they were kindred spirits, ready to explore. Though what he most hoped for, at the moment, was simply her reply . . . that his words had touched her heart . . . that she understood and felt the same.

Was he crazy? Daydreams were simplicity itself. He'd nearly forgotten she wasn't anywhere near. She was in Boston. Surrounded by an autumn landscape of towering trees, bright green leaves ready to turn red and gold, briny ocean air. The image was so spectacularly different from anything in these desert mountains that David was shocked into grappling with how infinitesimal the chances were that Amanda would feel anything about his letter except baffled. And how did he fancy they were going to walk these streets, hike the trails, stroll by the river? Even if the letter caught her attention, she had a life. Two thousand miles away. What did he think? That one letter would send her rushing back?

Until now, he had been so consumed with thoughts of her, he had been certain it would work out. Somehow. June apparently thought he and Amanda might be a match. But was he being ridiculous? Like usual? The truth was that loneliness often drove such wild imaginings. He always anticipated a happy ending. And he was always surprised when it failed. His heart had more cracks than spring ice.

Truth was, he hadn't dated that much. Mostly, he'd see a girl, develop a mad crush, and then imagine a romance to rival the movies. But girls seemed to shine a spotlight on his shyness. By the time he wrangled a date, the reality bore little resemblance to his embellished daydreams.

Every topic of conversation he thought up was dull. Every remark flat. Every compliment wanting. It shouldn't have been a surprise that all endings were nearly the same: The girls wanted to stay friends. Or they suddenly developed a boyfriend they'd forgotten to mention. Or, sometimes, the girls were so different from the way he had pictured them— they'd be petty, or catty, or so downcast they made him look like a live wire—that he'd wonder what could possibly have attracted him in the first place.

Could these crazy feelings for Amanda be just a long-distance production of that dreary drama? It was depressing to think so. Still, June, who knew Amanda better than anyone, had encouraged him to write. And Lionel thought it was a good letter and worth sending. It was amazing how comfortable David was with Lionel. Too bad girls couldn't be like that. Because, frankly, when he thought about loving someone, he imagined the kind of ease he felt with Lionel. He wanted that special someone, that radiant other, to be the kind of person he could share every insight with, every excitement and comfort. And she'd feel the same.

Coming up on his mother's house—a renovated adobe on Santa Fe's outskirts near the homes of several artists—he heard sounds of a party. His mother and her friends had been at the baile, and they excelled at protracted celebrations. Once inside, David could smell eggs and bacon. He poked his head into the kitchen just as Will Shuster was winding up what must have been a very long, very funny story. David shook his head at his mother's motion to join them, then navigated the dark, narrow hallway to his room. His spirits had lifted, the gaiety of his mother's party reigniting his hopes. He knew the letter was a shot in the dark. But it could still end well, couldn't it? Maybe Amanda would return to the Southwest. Finish college here. They'd take their time, fall in love. Eventually they'd send Lionel a postcard to thank him. They'd offer to name their first boy after him.

Drifting into sleep, smiling, David continued to construct his idea of a very happy ending. A telegram would arrive with instructions to meet the next train. Amanda would fall into his arms. And then—in that in-between state of wakefulness and sleep—he saw them sharing their innermost thoughts even though, immersed in conversation, he was also posting the letter. Hello? Amanda asked playfully. Remember me? Looking down, he realized he had crossed out Amanda's name and replaced it with Lionel's. Can't be helped, he told her, and pushed it into the mailbox anyway.

His eyes opened, stunned into wakefulness.

Geez, he thought. What was that about? Can't I at least be happy in my dreams? All I ask is something sweet, something simple. Give me that, he thought. But the hypnagogic vision of Lionel's name on the envelope prompted David to consider again that final ardent grip. This time, drowsily, he felt more curious than embarrassed. And then, slipping into unconsciousness, he wondered why it would have been wrong to just press back.

He is musing about this just as he realizes he's on the trail to Santa Fe Baldy in the Sangre de Cristo Range. At the summit, the entire earth arranges itself around him. To the north, the Truchas mountains. To the west, the Jemez. The Sandias to the south, the Rio Grande meandering toward Albuquerque. Spreading toward the east are the Las Vegas plains. Exhilarated, David lifts his arms to embrace his future. Then he turns toward home, but now the trail has so few markers, he has to consult a compass with a needle that refuses to settle, veering wildly in every direction. Just then, he hears Amanda calling from high in a ponderosa pine, nearly thirty feet up. He climbs from branch to branch to join her. "It was the letter," she says to him when he reaches her. "I had to be with you." David sits beside her and pulls her close. "This is it," he says to her. "This is what I want." He presses his lips into her hair, and then they share such an exquisite kiss David fears they may fall.

"Take the leap?" Amanda says. She grips his hand in hers—that electric shock!—and they fly from the branch, cartwheeling into an open meadow, embroidered with wildflowers. "We're meant for each other." It's a whisper in his ear as they tightly embrace in such a fever that David knows it must be love. Love *is* real, he thinks, and promises to follow wherever this takes him. He lifts his head to gaze into his lover's eyes only to find Lionel wrapped in his arms. Where's Amanda? he wonders, but the question vanishes like raindrops on a sunny day. Everything he wants is right here. I just need to say how much I love him, David thinks. He brushes his lips against Lionel's ear. "You're my love," he says. "Impossible to disguise." Lionel grips David's hand. This time, David squeezes back.

EIGHT

When Lionel followed June and David into St. Francis's parish hall, just around the corner from La Fonda, he did not need to fake surprise. The drab functional room had been transformed. June had mentioned Indian Fair earlier in the visit, but clearly Lionel had underestimated her description. The sheer number of pots impressed. At least five tiered tables, six feet wide and twenty feet long, were laden with pots, plates, and jars. Grouped by pueblo, earth-tone styles flowed around the room, surfacing as bold geometry, intricate meanders, wide-eyed birds.

The smell of scorched hide clung to one table, near where Lionel was standing. Along the center, towering over painted arrows, exquisitely beaded dolls, and hand-crafted knife sheaths, six ceremonial drums of varied sizes sat in a row. Crisscrossed cord, some with feathers, joined the drum leather at top and bottom. Lionel could only gawk. Overhead and along the walls, textiles hung, creating a bower of art. Some of the blanket patterns were so intricate they challenged the notion that humans were responsible. Others resembled pot designs, laid flat. Among the paintings on nearby walls were watercolors evoking dazzling Indian ceremonial dances with an abstract style that reminded Lionel of modernist galleries back east. A few paintings had been framed. Most were simply tacked to the wall.

While Lionel stood, thunderstruck, gazing about the room, June and David made their way toward the collection of San Ildefonso pots, a popular table. Lionel saw June point toward a pot, then tug on David's arm to lead him to another. Lionel also spotted Justin in the corner, viewing the paintings. Watching June's performance with David, Lionel wondered if she knew Justin was in the area. Lionel felt sure June had noticed Justin's changed behavior at the ball. After the photo, he had danced only once with Teresa and then seemed content to hand over ballroom duties to her brothers. Lionel guessed he was trying to puzzle out what was going on between June and David. Though once, looking up from the children's cape-and-bull game, Lionel had found Justin's eyes on him, practically glaring.

Lionel silently congratulated June on playing her part so well, especially since he was in a position to know that David was completely besotted with her, Amanda. Yet no one could be blamed for thinking that June and David really were in love. Watching him put his hand on June's elbow to steer around another couple leaning over the balustrade, Lionel unexpectedly revisited the shiver of excitement from grasping David's hand last night.

It was awfully tempting. What if everything were different? What would happen if she, Amanda, really were to say yes to David? The tingle of pleasure spread to the soles of her feet. Fiercely, Lionel commanded himself back to the present. He would spoil everything if he not only turned back into the giddy girl who had been left at the altar, but also managed to unmask himself here, now. Stay on course. Besides, he'd been tired and, probably, a little drunk. That zip of excitement? A mirage.

"Come see this plate," June said, appearing next to him. She pulled him toward the table and pointed to a large flat plate, twelve inches wide, glossy black. The design, also in black but with a matte finish, appeared as subtle grey. "Maria Martinez made that. Isn't it gorgeous?"

"It's similar to the pot I saw in La Fonda." He gazed at the design, a serpent circling the plate edge. "Everything here amazes me. It's outstanding."

"What's outstanding?" said Justin, approaching the railing.

"Maria's pottery," June answered and pointed. If she was unnerved by Justin's sudden appearance, she didn't give it away. "We're admiring that plate."

"Did you know her husband, Julian, actually paints the designs?" Justin said. "Maria makes the pots."

"Really?" Lionel asked June, who was pleased to be called on as an authority over Justin.

"Yes, Julian is the painter." She looked down the railing at Justin. "Nice of you to join us." June caught Lionel's eye and grinned. Justin registered the look, too—a look so intimate that he was positive he was on the right track about June and Lionel, though it made his heart lurch to think so.

Justin had been watching June closely ever since she and David had arrived. He was nowhere near ready to abandon his suspicions, despite what David had told him last night about seeing Lionel with Bob Hunt. He also could understand why David might have thought June was throwing herself at him. Frankly, it had been something of a shock to see her through another man's eyes . . . lovely girl, really, and a good listener, which he should know better than anyone.

But David and June were very old news, and Justin was certain nothing had changed. David and June had been friends too long. Instead Justin felt more and more sure that June's attention was simply a ploy to mask whatever was going on between her and Lionel. It made him feel left out and even more determined to discover the truth.

"And everything here has been entered for a prize?" Lionel asked, still directing questions to June.

"Yes, first and second prizes for each pueblo. Five dollars is first, right, David?"

"I think so," he said. He pointed across the room to a tall, lanky man dressed in a suit and wearing a hat, who was folding himself nearly in half to converse with one of the potters. "There's Mr. Chapman, who does all the judging. Well, the main judge anyway," David said. "I think he's talking to Tonita Roybal, from San Ildefonso." Thick, dark bangs shielded the woman's eyes. Her light-blue flowered cotton shift was covered by a purple-and-dark-blue stippled fabric draped across one shoulder and held in place at the waist by a string of silver disks. Soft leather boots covered her feet. David looked around the table and then spotted a red bowl, about eight inches in diameter, overlaid with a webbed black design. "That's one of hers, I'm pretty sure."

"Incredible," Lionel said, gazing for nearly a full minute. Then he moved along the railing, admiring more pottery, some like Maria's black-on-black plate, others with designs in black and red over beige. Further along, he pointed to two jars in glossy black with sculpted grooves, like spiraling waves. "I like those, too," he said.

"Those are melon jars," David said. "I don't know the name of the potter, though."

"Let me see if I can find out," June said, ready to circle around the others to get closer to where the volunteer art hostess was standing. Lionel was interested to note that the volunteer was deep in conversation with the famous Mr. Bynner. Ah, up early today, Lionel thought. And, apparently, not too much the worse for last night's wear. He would have preferred a sour, sickly Hal, but the memory of his success was still sweet, especially when Hal, noticing Lionel's eyes on him, scowled briefly before turning back to his conversation. Lionel searched the room for Bob Hunt, but without luck. Then he turned to the pots, wishing he could see the detail better. These glasses really were impossible for close ups. He decided to slip them off while everyone was watching June make her way toward the art hostess.

At that moment, June's path was interrupted by one of the artists.

"That pot?" he asked June, motioning toward the melon pots. "I heard you talking."

"Yes," June said. "Why, do you know the potter?" And then, observing him more closely while she waited for an answer, she added, tentatively, "Alfonso? Roybal?"

He broke into a grin. About ten years older than June and her friends, Alfonso wore a loose green shirt over grey work pants, his dark hair braided. When he noticed David standing with Lionel near the pots, his smile grew wider. "Mud people!" he said. "I am happy to see you!"

June looked toward David, perplexed. Mud people?

"Oh, I'm sorry," Alfonso said. "I just mean people with stuck car. In mud." But his eyes held laughter, thinking back to their meeting. He and his wife had been out with the wagon when they had come across three persons covered in mud: smeared across their faces, clumped in their hair, oozing between their toes. "Mud people!" Alfonso had told his wife in Tewa. "Must be left from the beginning of time." She had smiled indulgently at his joke. David, meanwhile, had squelched his way toward the wagon, displaying a fleck of mud on his front tooth at his hello. He had held out his hand to Alfonso, forgetting it too was caked in mud.

Climbing down from the cart, Alfonso had joined David where, both with crossed arms, they examined the scene. The car had been up to its axles in sticky clay, listing to the left, its back right side pointed toward the sky. It was the second time that day the car had been stuck. "You probably saw us pushing it," David had said. "It needs more traction." He had gestured behind him to the pile of rocks, half-buried in the mud, from their earlier effort. Then Alfonso looked ahead, beyond the bog.

"I could hitch the horses and pull." Alfonso said carefully, English clearly not his first language. "It's not far."

David had stalled a minute before answering, apparently torn between pride in wanting to finish the job himself and a desire to put the whole episode behind him. "Are you sure?" David said. "We won't be putting you out?"

"We can help. We're in no hurry. We're on our way back to Santa Clara. Been getting mud," Alfonso had said, pointing toward the back of the wagon, which had held a shovel and two mounds under a piece of canvas. "Safer inside the wagon than out, eh?" Alfonso had said. David had laughed. "We'll help the mud people," Alfonso had said to Serafina, switching to Tewa. "It should only take a minute." She had nodded, smiling. "I'll get the horses," Alfonso had said to

David. The car had been pulled onto dry land in a matter of minutes.

"But you are safe now, eh?" he said to June. "Walking in town is always safe."

June laughed. "Right you are. It's so nice to see you again. Let me make introductions. Re-make them, in some cases," she said, gesturing toward her friends. "I'm June Sheehan. And this is David Elliot, whom you have already met. And two other friends, Lionel Hairgrove and Justin Samuels."

"Ah yes," Alfonso said, nodding at David. "Man with the car." Alfonso faced Lionel, who was still holding his glasses and turning with a welcoming smile. "And we have met, too? Though you are having fun, dressed for Fiesta."

Lionel's smile remained fixed while he shoved his glasses back on, hoping no one else had seen. Meanwhile, he struggled to produce an appropriate response. David, buried in his own embarrassment over the episode of the stuck car, didn't seem to notice, but Justin noted Lionel's discomfort. Finally, Lionel stuttered, simply, "So nice to meet you," and held out his hand while June attempted to divert everyone's attention back to the pot.

"So, the pot? You know the potter?"

"Yes," he said. "And you know her. My wife, Serafina."

"Serafina! How wonderful! Remember, David?" June said. "We've all been admiring it."

"And that one, too," Alfonso said, pointing toward the smaller, rounder melon jar.

Lionel spoke up. "I was hoping to buy a pot. I'm here just for a few days, on my way to California. Are they for sale?"

"Yes. Serafina would like to sell them," Alfonso said.

"The big pot, four dollars. Small pot, three. The money is paid to the woman at the door," Alfonso said. He pointed to the cashier. "But the pot is not yours today. Tomorrow. You will be in Santa Fe?"

"For at least one more day," Lionel said. He turned back to the table, trying to decide between the two pots.

"Do you work on the pottery, too?" June asked. "We were just explaining to Lionel that Maria's pots are painted by her husband."

"I only drive the wagon for clay," Alfonso said. He faced the drawings on the wall and gestured. "I paint on paper."

"Really?" June said, walking closer to view the paintings. Justin followed, leaving Lionel and David to contemplate the pottery. "This is yours?" Alfonso stood in front of a watercolor of a rainbow-colored eagle hovering over a deer and its fawn.

"It's beautiful!" June said, examining it. A blue ribbon and a SOLD sign had been tacked alongside the painting. She and Justin stepped closer to admire the detail.

David, left alone with Lionel, wasn't sure whether to follow. June would probably want him to stick with her to continue the charade. But he didn't feel up to more conversation with Alfonso. He knew he was in Alfonso's debt, but he was too uncomfortable about the car episode.

On the other hand, embarrassment over a car might be preferable to standing alone next to Lionel. All day, his brain had roiled with confusion. After the excitement of posting the letter to Amanda last night, his first thought this morning had been of . . . Lionel. He'd awakened from a dream of being with Lionel in the wilderness, where they had been close . . . so close. The thought made him squirm. Even though in the dream, it had seemed perfect. When he tried to imagine where that dream had come from, he could point only to being able to share things with Lionel that he would never have mentioned to any other guy. Imagine asking Justin to read one of his love letters! But that was all that had happened between them. Right?

Yet now the romantic fantasies about Amanda that had swarmed in his brain for the past several days seemed to have vanished, incredibly. In the daylight, her existence seemed like a mirage. He could hardly believe he had posted that letter. Not that she would ever reply. At least he wouldn't have to worry about seeing her. The whole idea of a future together seemed preposterous. What had he been thinking? It was best to forget. He'd just add her to his long list of lost opportunities and ill-suited fantasies. No harm done.

Now, these thoughts about Lionel . . . that was crazy. Yet, even with that notion flitting through his mind, he caught sight of Hal Bynner, chatting with one of the potters and turning David's every picture of himself on its head. It was absurd. He had never been attracted to any of his school friends. He did not intend to start now. It was as fantastic an idea as he'd ever had. But standing so close to Lionel, remembering the jolt of excitement he'd felt during that final handshake, a kernel of a truth tore at his heart.

The object of his confusion was concentrating on the pots, apparently trying to decide between them but also acutely aware of being alone with David, their hands inches apart on the railing. Say something, Lionel ordered himself. Anything. Just get your mind off the urge to brush your fingers against his. "I enjoyed our talk," he finally blurted.

"Ah, me, too," said David. How ridiculous! He was glowing, knowing Lionel thought well of him. "But listen to this, will you? When I woke up this morning, I couldn't help feeling the letter was a mistake. I mean, gee, she lives thousands of miles away." He knew he should have kept his mouth shut, but something made him want to confide. Too late, he realized what he had just said.

Lionel, mouth open, managed to shut it. What the hell? "I'm sorry," he said stiffly. "I seemed to have given you bad advice." He nervously smoothed his mustache. What did David mean? Had he given up? How could that be? If there was anything in the world to count on, it was that David knew himself to be in love with Amanda.

"No, of course not," David said miserably. So much for Lionel thinking well of him. "Really. I can't thank you enough for the time you spent listening to me. I know how I sounded. I'm as surprised as anyone that I'm having second thoughts about mailing it."

"So it's in the mail?" Lionel said, unexpectedly relieved. "I wouldn't worry then. You may be surprised, David."

"That's what I'm afraid of."

"Of being surprised?"

"Of having started something that, well, maybe I don't want to finish. Gosh, I barely know the girl."

Lionel stared.

"I know how that sounds. But I was a little hasty, is all," David continued, only too aware that his and Lionel's shoulders were nearly touching. It was agonizing to look at him, so David gazed across the hall where, once again, his eyes found Hal, now in close conversation with Bob Hunt, who had just arrived and was leading them toward one of the blankets on the wall. Lionel, following his gaze, seemed also to notice Hal and friend. David looked away.

"I dropped the letter in the mail slot at the post office

after we talked last night," David said. "But everything looked different this morning. You know?" He forced himself to look at Lionel, concentrating on his glasses. "I don't know what got into me. I think it was just a crush. Lord knows why it seemed so important." He shook his head and dropped his eyes to stare again at his hands, now tight around the railing.

"You've had a change of heart?" Lionel asked. He had stopped looking at Hal and Bob, and he could hear a falter in his own voice. David shot him a quick glance. Listening to Bynner continue to expound on his reasons for admiring the blanket seemed to give David a little courage.

"After I got home last night, with the letter mailed, I was just consumed with thoughts about love and what it means. What I want. What I hope for. I could barely sleep. I realized I'm past the stage of crushes. I want more than daydreams. I want someone real, someone to talk with. Someone I can say anything to."

"Well, sure," Lionel said, astonished. "So you've said. But that's where Amanda comes in, right? I read your letter. Wasn't that why you were so attracted?"

David's face twisted in misery. "I thought so. But this morning . . ." He had been trying to make peace with that foolish dream all day. Everything about the past two days looked different now, especially Lionel. He was certain the dream had been nudging him toward a truth. Was the way he had felt in the dream the reason he was always chasing, but never finding, love? "I guess I just was faced with reality. Gosh, I spent an afternoon with Amanda and didn't say more than two words to her. It was a pipe dream. About someone who lives half the country away, for heaven's sake. I believed in it. You know I did. But now I feel like there was nothing there after all, just me all caught up in a fantasy. As usual." He grew still. His promise in the dream—to follow his feelings—emerged with perfect clarity. He must act. If anyone could make sense of this, it would be Lionel. "And, well, I've begun to think about someone else. Someone who makes me really appreciate what love could be like, real love. Someone who understands me. Someone I can say *anything* to." Lord, he hoped he wasn't going to regret this. But if it was meant to be, if this was really who he was, then surely Lionel would understand what he was trying to say. Lionel had much more experience in this area. At least he could give David a sign?

Lionel, momentarily shocked into silence, simply continued staring at the pots without recognition. David drew hope from the pause. Finally recovering, Lionel said, "Well, old man, it's hard to keep up with you. Tell me. Who is this new flame?"

The detachment in his tone chilled David. "No one you know," David stammered. "I mean, I don't really think I should say." Lionel hadn't understood a word. David's heart sank, and he swore never to say another word. And yes, regrets were already surging. He seemed to be getting more dim-witted by the minute. It was a relief that June and the others were headed back to the table.

"Did you decide, Lionel?" June said. "Let me guess. I bet you picked the smaller bowl. Not for the price," she said hastily, making sure Alfonso wouldn't take offense. "But Lionel's traveling."

"Absolutely right, as usual, June," said Lionel, uttering the first thing that came to mind. "The smaller bowl will be easier to pack, but that's not why I chose it. Sometimes art just calls to you. Do you know what I mean?" Lionel looked at June, now with David at her side. Was June the reason for David's sudden mood swing? June tucked her arm into David's, smiling.

"Excellent choice," David said, forcing a hearty tone.

"Write down the number," Justin said to Lionel. "We'll take it to the cashier by the door."

"I will come too," Alfonso said. "To answer any questions." He and Lionel walked off together toward the cashier.

"Well, did he convince you?" June said to David, as they left.

"Convince me of what?" David said, startled.

"To mail that letter to Amanda," June said. "Isn't that what you've been talking about?"

"I mailed it last night," David snapped. "Big mistake. Thanks for reminding me."

"David!"

"I'm sorry," he said, massaging his temple with the heel of his hand. "Hangover."

They stood together in silence until the others returned. Lionel couldn't help noticing their closeness, nor June's concern.

"Please tell Serafina how much I admire the bowl," Lionel said to Alfonso abruptly, suddenly anxious to leave. When he had first spotted Hal and Bob in the hall, he had thought about seeing if he could create a little more mischief. Last night, it had worked so well. But now, confused by the conversation with David, he was overwhelmed by a need to get away. "I'll be back tomorrow to pick it up and hope to see you again." He told June, "Thanks awfully for bringing me to the fair. But if you don't mind, I'm going to have to leave. Professor Darnelle and his wife asked me to spend time with them this afternoon."

"Of course, Lionel," June said. "I'm so happy you were able to see all this. And I know you chose the right pot."

"Always nice to see you, Lionel," Justin said, adding, "Enjoy your time with the professor."

"Thank you," Lionel said.

"Oh, just one minute, Lionel," June said, as he started to walk away. What now? Lionel thought. "I forgot to ask . . . would you care to join David, Justin, and me for the Hysterical Parade? Tomorrow? It's going to be such fun. Teresa will be in it."

"Be honest, June," Justin said. Lionel held his breath, but all he heard next was, "We have an ulterior motive, Lionel. La Fonda is the best place to see the parade, and as a guest, you'll have a great view from the roof. So, if we could join you . . ."

"Are we being pushy?" June asked.

Lionel knew he should say no, but he was feeling so confused and bewildered by David he didn't dare invent anything. Better just say yes. There'd be time between now and then to untangle it all. Besides, he still had a duty to June, didn't he? Find out more about Justin? Though he wondered if June even cared anymore.

"It's the least I can do," he said. "Why don't you all stop by my room? When does it start?"

"The parade begins at four," June said. "Could we meet around three thirty?"

"It's a date," said Justin, speaking for them all. "See you tomorrow, Lionel. And perhaps the professor, too!"

NINE

Amanda walked away from the hall, caring little about which way she was headed. The professor. What had made her use him as an excuse? She had to have the slowest wit in the world. David's change of heart had her completely disoriented. What could have happened? Last night, he was gushing praise for her. Now? It was just a little crush. It must be June, she thought. David falling in love with her was the only thing that made sense.

Ignoring the niggle of pain that struck her heart when she imagined them together, she tried on logic. She had no claims on David. She didn't really want him. Or anyone for that matter. She should be pleased for June, who not only wanted love, but deserved it more than most, even if Justin had always been too dense to see it. Now, thanks to Amanda, June's many fine qualities were suddenly crystal clear . . . to David. Really, if the news stung, she had no one to blame but herself. She should have been far more diligent in following up with Justin. Hadn't she promised? But at the baile last night and Indian Fair today, she had allowed herself to be distracted. Perhaps June would be hanging on Justin's arm right now if Lionel had been more conscientious.

On the other hand, what was June up to? Had it slipped her mind to tell Amanda that, oh, by the way, she had given up on Justin? Was she deep in the throes of real love, now that David had fallen for her? Or did she still pine for Justin, and so would be sure to disappoint David in the end? Imagining David forlorn and free made Amanda's heart quicken. Then she felt worse. Honestly, she chided. Two weeks ago, she had arrived in Santa Fe, determined to find herself. And here she was. On her own and better for it. It's what she wanted. Besides, if she ever again even *considered* falling in love, why would she think twice about a boy as a fickle as David? If he now found himself in love with June, well, best of luck to them.

The problem she should be working on was how to get through that fool parade tomorrow. How had she ended up agreeing to host the whole group at La Fonda? Including David and June. This time loss enveloped Amanda, aches snaking along every limb. That damn letter. At this very minute, it was speeding its way toward her Boston address. Every word intended for her, Amanda. How could David act now as if it meant nothing? Did he peel off soulful letters like grocery lists?

Consumed with questions and disagreeable answers, Amanda found herself standing in La Fonda's lobby. She slumped into a chair that faced the patio where, against the adobe wall, hollyhocks in every shade of red grew on stalks as tall as a man. Pulling a book from a stack on the table next to her, Amanda tried to focus on the open page, but all she could think about was that damn letter. It had reached into places so private, it had undermined every defense. Because she might as well admit it. Until that letter, she had slammed the door on love, turned her back, crossed her arms, and stood firm. But with that letter—she'd lost her heart. What she had struggled so long to see about herself, David had captured in two pages. Pain coursed anew. David and June? How had she let it happen? She forced herself to sit up and, desperate to ignore the hurt, began to read from the page of poetry open in her lap.

> The plums and cherries are blossoming,
> My heart, too, is unsheathing from winter—
> And it has all happened in one day.

Tears welled, black type shimmering on the page. The poet could have been writing her. Pure genius, whoever it was. She flipped to the cover. *A Canticle of Pan* by Witter Bynner. Surely not! Hal? She recoiled slightly, tears drying, and reread the poem, looking for hints of wicked intent. But the poem persisted in its beautiful expression. He knew.

Well, fine. So he knew a little bit about love's transformation. Probably every human being who had ever fallen for somebody knew about that. It didn't pardon his unspeakable sin of ridiculing Mabel and her efforts to break society from its shackles, did it? She was sure it did not and that she'd been right to seek revenge. Besides, that poem was a lucky chance. Hal's other poems would not speak to her so clearly. She turned the page:

> Out of a fairy-tale they flew above me,
> Three white wild swans with silk among their wings—
> And one might be a princess and might love me,
> If I had not forgotten all such things

> They flew abreast and would not pause nor quicken,

One of them guarded by the other two,
And left me helpless here, alone and stricken,
Without the secret that I thought I knew.

She slammed the book on the table, causing a middle-aged couple, who had been deep in conversation, to look over in amazement from across the room. "So sorry," she muttered, then grabbed a magazine from the pile, opening it at random, her thoughts a jumble of confusion. Oh, this whole adventure was beginning to unravel. If she was smart, she'd walk upstairs, pack her bags, and take the next train out of here. She had learned a thing or two about herself. Call it victory and leave. Besides, if June had truly fallen for David, what reason was there now for Amanda to stay? Setting the magazine down, on the verge of heading upstairs to pack, Amanda spied Mabel's byline on the open page. It was a short article about the creative impulse. Amanda sat back down, amazed. What had Mabel said so often? Let it happen. Let the great force behind the scenes direct the action.

Ten minutes later, Amanda stared bleakly out the patio window, sitting as still as possible. The only word she could summon was "bereft." It occurred to her that she had felt like this for a long, long time. Her summer's quest, she thought now, had been all diversion. Admitting to the emptiness seemed like the most genuine emotion she'd had in months.

For Mabel's guidance had not cast the magic of old. Instead, as Amanda had scanned eagerly for hints about next steps, the world had tipped. Staring out now, Amanda was surprised that the patio hollyhocks still remained upright, cherry and pink, fluttering in the breeze. Because, there on the page, blared nearly the same words Mrs. Shee-han had used days—it seemed like months—ago. Mabel's need to interfere in people's lives. Her belief that creativity was a man's domain. Her self-absorption. In the article, Mabel celebrated the female's ability to love, nurture, and intuit . . . as a means of inspiring society's great male talents. To illustrate, she had described her own experience with D. H. Lawrence who, Amanda recalled, was the author of books so racy that Wellesley girls had passed on censored editions of *Women in Love* with more vigilance than shots of whiskey. He was one of the truly "great souls" that Mabel had willed to New Mexico. Lawrence and his wife, Frieda, had recently settled in Taos at her urging. Mabel looked on Lawrence as the instrument necessary to establish her vision of the Southwest as a center for social and psychic renewal. She reveled in her power as muse. She even admitted, in paragraph six, that he was meant to take *her* experience, *her* material, *her* Taos, and manifest it as a magnificent creation. She saw it as her duty to seduce Lawrence's spirit, his cre-ative imagination, his genius—Amanda doubted it had stopped there—so Mabel could use his soul for the highest purpose.

Mabel's own words. Amanda sat, dazed, the article clutched in her hand. The world had not only tipped, but twisted. In little more than an hour, all she had believed in had been proven a sham. Again. And again. And again. David. Hal. Mabel. She felt unmoored.

And without the secret she thought she knew.

Air. She needed air. Throwing the magazine onto the table, she whipped out the door, past the Plaza, headed who knows where for the second time that day. If she was lucky—very lucky—she'd walk so darned fast, she could leave these thoughts in the dust. Everything felt like a fraud. Her focus on self-discovery. Her allegiance to Mabel. Her confidence that she—alone!—knew the secret to creating an authentic life. Embarrassment crowded out all other emotions as she recalled her conduct over the summer, especially these past weeks in Santa Fe. What arrogance. And self-absorption! What must June and the others have thought about this mixed-up girl with all the answers? They had been too tolerant by far. And David! He actually said he admired her stupid quest. He must be as loopy as she was. Thank god she was leaving. Once she was home, she'd throw his letter in the trash and hope never again to hear his name.

And, oh my god, Hal—she saw herself back in the hall, urging Bob to leave on a walk, and her thrill at Hal's wounded look when they had returned. She was as bad as Mabel, messing with people's lives like that. She would need to make amends. Somehow. But losing Mabel. Here, Amanda felt a hole in her heart as big as the moon. When she had latched on to Mabel's philosophy, it had seemed as solid as an oak. Now, its own weight had caused it to fall, crashing into boulders on its way down, leaving only broken pieces littering the ground. How would Amanda find her way without Mabel as a guide?

By this time, her route had brought her to Montezuma Lodge, where she became aware of a humming. It intensified as she continued past the lodge's pink walls and up the hill. At the top, the new bowl-shaped Fiesta Theater abruptly came into view and the humming transformed itself into Indian songs. From where she was standing, Amanda could look into the open theater and make out lines of dancers. Crowds were still filtering in, although the performance had already begun. Impulsively, Amanda decided to look for a seat near the back. The theater was nothing more than benches, arranged on one side of a partially cleared hillside, looking down toward the bottom of a bowl where the dancers were. A dozen pairs of men and women moved in unison, bodies erect, arms held close. The men sang as they danced. The women's eyes, cast down, seemed fixed on their wrapped boots, which lifted slightly on each *tap*-tap.

The view from the benches not only looked down on the dancers but also took in the surrounding countryside, including nearby residences clustered below small bluffs. Plateaus stretched into the distance, with the Jemez peaks beyond. Billowing masses of clouds, grey like the sea, threw the area into deep shadow and threatened thunderstorms. Onstage, the dancers flowered like blooms in a darkened room. Squash blossom necklaces glittered on dark wool dresses. Vividly embroidered sashes secured lace-trimmed shawls, draped over each woman's shoulder. The women held spruce boughs in their right hands, woven baskets in their left. The men, shirtless, wore embroidered blankets like kilts. Gourd rattles in their right hands rhythmically accompanied the song, with spruce boughs gripped in their left. Dark braids hung below elaborate headdresses. Circles of feathers fluttered in bands around the men's upper arms, elbows, and neck. Bells jangled at their ankles.

Amanda, practically oblivious to the scene, continued looking inward, locked into recycling her internal litany of blame. Over and over, she revisited how badly she had acted. How grossly she had misjudged everyone. How worthless it had been to follow Mabel. How everything she had learned was rubbish. And how, by emulating Mabel, Amanda had become a meddler, just like her. How unfair she had been to Hal. Clearly, Mabel laid herself open to ridicule. Because of her fierce loyalty to Mabel, Amanda had felt justified in inserting jealousy into Hal's love life. It might have flourished but for her. Maybe it was her punishment that she now suffered in the same way, fearful she had lost a potential friend and partner who had seen her as she was and—most amazingly—had valued her for it. She thought about packing and train schedules and how to get word to June. She imagined how she would feel when she was back at Wellesley. She tried to frame words that could explain herself.

Patiently, in spite of everything, the dance began to penetrate her consciousness and crowd out the reproaches. Without realizing it, she began to react, first as an onlooker, then as participant, even though she remained in her seat, riveted by the scene. The women were kneeling now, repeatedly scraping sticks over their baskets, unloosing an eerie drone. The men's singing, which had sounded monotonous to Amanda's ears initially, quietly transformed itself into the beat of her own heart. Time seemed suspended, as if the moment stretched back all the way to the birth of the mountain ridges looming in the distance.

Amanda had to shake herself back into the world when the dance ended. The sight of the audience—the boys' baggy plus fours, the men's wide-legged trousers, the women's waistless chemises and cloche hats—appeared as strange to Amanda as if she had awakened into science fiction. More startling were her own pair of pants, not to mention the feathery mustache tickling her nose. She turned to others, hoping to bond over the shared experience, but most seemed unaware of the effect. Kids pestered their parents for popcorn. Men sized up the possibilities for World Series contenders. Other dancers, waiting for their turn, were talking among themselves, lifting drums, adjusting arm-bands.

She turned to the program in her hand, trying to regain her sense of place, and read about the basket dance as an invocation of fertility. Still affected by the meditative aspects of the dance, she was suffused with feelings of acceptance and continuity, feelings—she remembered with a shock—that Mabel had written about. In one of her articles, Mabel had described the freshness of Pueblo dances as being like the water of a bottomless spring—ever new, yet forever the same. It irked Amanda to be aligned with Mabel, even in shared recognition of the beauty of the basket dance. She preferred to discredit that idea—any idea, if it were Mabel's. It upset her that she had to admit its truth . . . because that was how the dance had felt.

Yet being sympathetic to Mabel's ideas dismayed her. Mabel had proven herself unworthy. Therefore, Amanda was positive she wanted no part of her. Or almost positive. What she craved most was clarity. Choosing to discard Mabel, labeling her a worthless person, that would give Amanda back a sense of certainty, wouldn't it? Mabel's own words had exposed her as less than perfect, so Amanda should feel free to turn her back on her—Amanda's choice of action, it seemed—rather than being forced to account for actual insights Mabel had uncovered. Because . . . how could Amanda be expected to hold two opposite points of view at once?

Onstage, a new dance had begun. Six singers and a drummer stood stage right. A single dancer in the center of the stage, clothed in red and black, was already in motion, drawing his knees higher than his waist in rhythm to the song. Amanda could see from her program that he was from Taos and performing the hoop dance, a sort of healing ceremonial representing the circle of life. This time, Amanda welcomed the chance to leave her thoughts behind and engage with the steady, strong beat of the drum, the prayerful chants, and the dancer's fluid form.

At the start, the pattern was simple—steps in and out of several hoops like a child at hopscotch. But the speed of the hoop dancer's footwork increased until his fast, sure movements blurred the beads and feathers on his crimson-colored shirt and vest. Small bells on his leggings sang like birds. Kicking up one hoop, the dancer became enveloped by the circle, which traveled up and down his body like water. Locking two hoops onto his arms, then three, the dancer grew wings across his back. The hoops fluttered into the air, then down with the beat of the drum. The hoops were in constant motion, suddenly expanding so that where there had been three, now there were five, then seven, intricately patterned to mimic the flight of an eagle. Other transformations followed—the hoops became a butterfly, a turtle, the earth. Amanda felt her own body strain to imitate the dancer's movements, yearning to capture not only his agility but also the threads of enchantment.

Focused on the dancer's impossible feats, she dared to think that if a hoop dancer were faced with her current confusion, he would not retreat. He would step in and around it, letting it transform itself, until each event had been translated. He'd accept those opposite truths until they fit together like hoops into wings. The dance's promise of innovation and continuity revealed a novel approach, encouraging Amanda to change perspective. Accept the complexity of those around her. Give up her need to make life into a prescriptive list. Abandon rigid judgments. There'd be no more turning her back. No more black and white. Just acceptance of gradations. And not always grey. She'd let in every color of the rainbow.

When the dancer ended the performance by coiling several hoops on each arm in dizzy splendor, Amanda joined with the crowd in crying out her appreciation, receptive to the spirit of the dance, hoping to make it her own.

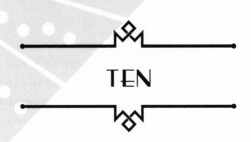

TEN

Justin knocked smartly on the door. Lionel opened immediately, as if standing on the other side, and was surprised to see only Justin. He looked down the hall and found David, arm in arm with June, inspecting artwork on the walls. His heart skipped. Justin moved to enter the room, but Lionel quickly pulled the door shut. "We'd better go right to the roof for a good spot," he said, leading them all down the corridor to the stairwell. Already, a steady stream of people was climbing the stairs.

Hanging back with David to allow June to climb the steps before them, Lionel wondered how he was going to manage the next couple of hours. It was the first time he'd seen David since he—well, Amanda—had admitted to love.

Yesterday, the exhilaration from the hoop dance had buoyed Amanda, despite a thorough drenching on the walk back—as if the dances had summoned the showers— sending everyone dashing for shelter. When the worst had passed, Amanda had returned to La Fonda for dry clothes, then decided to remain in the room even after Fiesta resurrected itself. Lying on the bed, listening to words from a hundred different conversations drifting in the window, and smelling the blossom-sweet rain-soaked air, Amanda had been reminded of earlier that summer in Boston, when she had spent so much time in her room. But this time she felt different. More resilient. Whatever else she could say about this visit, she knew she was stronger.

The evening had given her time to think, trying to reconcile all she had learned—and unlearned—at the dances. She searched for balance. Mabel, Hal, David. Repelled by Mabel's manipulations, Amanda's unthinking loyal allegiance had disappeared for good. But Mabel's brilliance! What to do with that? Her writing, her insights. Her single-minded attempts to grab life and shake it into a glorious concoction that would save the world. How to reconcile the richness life had revealed since Amanda had been introduced to Mabel's ideas, with the paucity of Mabel's petty desires? Somehow, Amanda knew, she would have to teach herself how to live with messiness. How to make blurred hoops into wings.

And Hal. Guilt pricked at Amanda like the barbed hairs on a prickly pear. Her behavior at the baile in defense of—now she knew—feet-of-clay Mabel appalled her. Arrogance. Again. At the time, it had seemed so important to take revenge because . . . why? Because Hal was a shrewd writer? A creator of witty farce? And then, when she'd discovered his poetry reflecting her emotions like a mirror . . . Trying to keep perspective, she realized she still didn't know him well. Perhaps Hal's own feet were dusted with terra-cotta. But she knew neither he nor Bob had deserved her interference. How could she fix it? All of her ideas just seemed like more meddling, curdling her heart.

Finally, David. Amanda divided her time that evening between self-recrimination and hopeful scenarios. The puzzle of David's new love consumed her. Was it June? If not, then who? And how could anyone be a better match for David than Amanda? And how was she ever going to find out? Should she stay in town? Should she remain in disguise? Every question hammered her head without mercy or hope of resolution.

The following morning, her queries still without answers, Amanda had remembered Serafina's pot. Waiting in line at the hall, her eyes had strayed to the spot where David had confessed his changed feelings. Recalling his vehemence, Amanda's hopes had shriveled into dry stalks. Despondent, she was surprised by Alfonso joining her in line, there to retrieve some unsold paintings. Wanting to set the record straight, and with nothing to lose, Amanda had taken off her glasses, pretending to examine the pot more closely, and then looked up, hopeful, into Alfonso's eyes. "Stuck in mud!" Alfonso had said. Amanda had laughed her own, genuine laugh. "You were right," Amanda had said. "The costume is just some Fiesta fun." While they had talked, her relief in admitting the charade—and Alfonso's crinkled smile—overwhelmed her. Maybe she'd have the same luck with David. She made up her mind then to stay at least through the parade. It would give her time to discover if David and June really were in love. If they were . . . well, she would signal June to look for a message in the hidden rock and call it quits. There was a train out tonight, and her suitcase was packed. She had already written a note, wishing them the best. She just had to discover the truth and make peace with the answer. Somehow.

On La Fonda's roof, most of the crowd clustered near the edge, looking down San Francisco Street toward the cathedral. June and David were trying to make a space among everyone there. Lionel hung back with Justin. Excited voices sparked the air, interrupted by laughter, with nearly everyone in a fever pitch over Fiesta's last day. But Lionel couldn't find it in himself to join in. Despite a resolve to accept the truth—whatever it might be—the sight of June placing her hand lightly on David's arm while they edged toward the roof wall made his heart plunge. Then he noticed Justin also focusing on June's arm, before sighing and turning to Lionel.

"Are Professor Darnelle and his wife going to be here?" Justin asked.

"I'm afraid not," Lionel answered, thankful for an answer he had prepared last evening. "The professor's real interest is history, so he was only here for the pageants. We said good-bye yesterday."

"I see," Justin said slowly, as if looking for a hole in Lionel's story and a bit disappointed to find none. He covered by launching into the very short history of the Hysterical Parade—created only this year by Santa Fe's artists to spoof Fiesta's historical aspects—but June interrupted.

"We just caught sight of Teresa's float," June told them. "Well, we think so, anyway. You should see it, Lionel. It's covered with tissue flowers in just about every color you can imagine. We helped with it a little," she said, pointing to David.

"Teresa's in the parade?" Lionel asked. But that was hardly his real concern. It had only now occurred to him that by staying in last night, he'd given June and David even more time on their own.

"Yes, and on such short notice, too," Justin said. "Though all the groups around town tried to have a float. Right, June?" But she was already back by David's side, looking down directly onto the street. Justin frowned.

"I've been meaning to ask," Lionel said quietly to Justin, deciding to grab his chance while they were out of hearing of the others. Better late than never, he thought. "How's forbidden fruit?" He smiled. "You and Teresa did make a lovely couple at the dance."

But Justin's attention was on June, who was laughing with David about something on the street. Justin then looked directly at Lionel. "Speaking of lovely couples," he said and nodded toward David and June.

For a moment, Lionel, flustered, was incredulous that Justin had somehow intuited his distress over David. Was he a mind reader? Or, worse, had he uncovered the disguise? Searching for a fitting response while trying to discern what Justin knew—and for how long—it suddenly dawned on him that Justin was trying to discover if Lionel was upset by seeing *June* with someone else. Oh, if you only knew, Lionel thought.

"They do seem happy," Lionel said, in a tone he trusted was suitably detached. "June is looking especially lovely, isn't she?" Truly, June could have reigned as Fiesta queen. Dressed in the pink-and-black gown she had worn at the baile and animated by all the festivities of Fiesta's final day, she positively radiated sex. Though maybe it wasn't just the dress or Fiesta, Lionel thought. Maybe it was love. Justin and Lionel were both silent, staring at David and June, when she turned and called them over. "Come see this little dog," she said. "It's dressed up like a burro!"

Down on San Francisco Street, crowds lined both sides,

with more than half of the spectators in some kind of costume. Even staid businessmen peered out from under sombreros. A huge number of celebrants had gathered in the Plaza itself, many waiting for the floats to appear while they stood in line at impromptu food stands. Although a police officer was encouraging everyone to stay out of the street because the parade was expected shortly, he couldn't control a Labrador mix, weaving in and out of the crowds and sporting a burro's tall ears, short mane, and feather-duster tail.

Lionel, catching sight of it, laughed along with the others. They were crammed together. Sneaking a glance at David, he was relieved to see that, despite the witty dog-burro, he looked more like a man under strain than one in love. Maybe, Lionel thought wistfully, he was still thinking about Amanda, finding it difficult to choose between her and June. Their proximity was tantalizing. He leaned around David to look toward the cathedral and they brushed shoulders. Ah, forbidden fruit. He was beginning to see the attraction. The slightest touch launched shivers. But then Lionel cursed himself. Hadn't he just resolved never again to interfere in anyone's life? And messing with David meant messing with June. David's hands were on her waist while she leaned over the wall, attempting to catch the first glimpse of the parade. Was David just playing along? Or was the intimacy genuine? Lionel realized he would never know the truth by looking. He was going to have to get June alone and ask.

Someone on the roof called out that they could see the parade leaders—petite Dolly Sloan and towering Hal Bynner—and all heads turned toward the corner near the cathedral. Lionel felt another pang of guilt at the sight of

Hal. He hadn't yet decided how he was going to make it up to him. But guilt and love sickness were no match for the outright silliness of the parade. Following Dolly and Hal was the Conquistadores' Band, so ubiquitous during Fiesta events that they seemed like wizards, appearing and disappearing at will. After them, strung out in a procession a mile long, were floats and costumes that skewered the very history Santa Fe was supposed to be celebrating. Exploding biscuits punched the air from "La Funny's" kitchen float. King Ferdinand and Queen Isabella waved to their subjects from stately thrones. Behind them, three separate clotheslines on which hung several pairs of enormous pants and shirts—the pant legs were at least three feet wide—swayed down the street. After them, Peeping Tom led a huge white horse on which rode Lady Godiva, whose costume consisted of little white shorts. ("That's really John Windsor," June explained to Lionel, laughing.) Everyone in town with a horse or burro was in the parade, sporting cowhand outfits and riding ahead of dozens of loaded wood wagons. June let out an unladylike whoop— half-laughing as she looked back in alarm at Lionel—as soon as she spotted Teresa on the Centre de Cultura's floating piñata. ("We were right about that float, David," June said.) At the parade's end, students and staff from the Los Alamos Boys Ranch traveled in a dude pack train of fifty horses, toting every tenderfoot comfort from three-course meals to bathtubs.

By the time the last float passed by, the four were arguing good-naturedly over which was the best. David and Lionel defended the dude pack train, Justin argued for the clothesline, and June loyally stood up for Teresa's piñata. Out in the street, David and Justin continued the argument as they joined a crowd on Shelby Street heading toward St. Michael's for the bullfight and polo game.

"Hang back a little, won't you, June?" whispered Lionel, catching her arm and letting several people crowd in front of them as they passed the garage on Water Street. "I was hoping we could talk."

"Isn't Fiesta the best?" June said, oblivious to Lionel's anxiety. "Though if it went on much longer, I'd probably die from lack of sleep."

"Oh?" asked Lionel.

"I've been out every night since it began," June said. "It's too bad you couldn't be with us through all of it. But I know the disguise puts a strain on you. Though you're carrying it off beautifully. I really don't think anyone has had even a moment's suspicion."

Lionel was less certain—Justin was suspicious, even if he didn't yet seem close to the real answer. But no time for that now. He and June might be alone only for a minute or two. Surprising even himself, he blurted out, "Are you in love with David?"

June stopped so suddenly that a teenaged boy and girl, holding hands, bumped right into her. "Beg your pardon," the boy muttered. He and his girlfriend unlocked their hands to step around them, then fell back together just ahead. June burst out laughing. "My goodness," she said. "Are you serious?"

"Absolutely serious," Lionel said, annoyed.

"Well, that's perfect then," June said, smiling contentedly. "I mean, if you can even ask the question, knowing what you do . . . well, what must Justin think?"

Breathing a huge sigh of relief at the mention of Justin's name, Lionel felt more confident about continuing. "So you're not in love with David? You still have feelings for Justin?" They had started walking again.

"Of course," June said, who now look puzzled. "It was your idea. What are you thinking?"

"Oh, June, I don't know what to think," Lionel said. "It's just, well . . . I can't believe I'm going to say this to you . . . but I think I'm in love with David."

"You are!" cried June. "I'm so happy. You know he's crazy about you."

"Was," Lionel said. "Was crazy about me."

"Was? What do you mean?"

"I found out yesterday. At Indian Fair. Remember when you and Justin went to look at Alfonso's painting? David and I had a chance to talk . . . and he told me he'd met someone. Not Amanda. Someone who made him finally realize what love is," Lionel said sadly. It sounded even worse out loud. "I think he means you."

"Oh, for goodness' sake," June said. "I can't believe it. I haven't felt anything like that. And David hasn't mentioned a thing," she continued. The boys were still several yards ahead of them. They had crossed Alameda and were continuing down College Street, although they might turn any moment. "Honestly, who could it be? He and I have been together practically every minute for nearly three days."

"You don't think it's you? Really?"

June shook her head.

"It couldn't be Teresa, could it?" Lionel ventured.

"Teresa! Oh, my goodness. Now that would be a twist. But no, I don't think so. David was with me, even at the baile. If anyone spent time with Teresa, it was Justin." June suddenly looked stricken. "Though, come to think of it, it was David's idea to help Teresa last night with some last-minute decorations for the float." She groaned. "Oh, Lionel, I just can't imagine it. And, honestly, even though Justin had been making a fool of himself over Teresa, I had a chance to talk with her. She's as steadfast as can be about Christopher."

"Well, that's good news," Lionel said, but now he was busy trying to reconstruct every memory he had of David and Teresa together. He wished he had known this before the parade. He would have paid more attention to David's expression when Teresa's float passed below. Instead he had been concentrating on Justin, who, surprisingly, had given Teresa barely a glance, before turning his attention back to June. "I don't know what to say. You should have heard David at Indian Fair. He is passionate about this girl, whoever she is. Are you sure it isn't you?"

"If it is, it's well hidden. As far as I can tell, he's just playing along, like I asked. He even told me that he thinks Justin's finally sitting up and taking notice, and that he hoped we'd have a happy ending to that story very soon. Gosh, and I thought everything was going so well."

"It is!" Lionel said. "Well, that part, anyway. I should have told you right away—Justin really did have his eye on you and David. And he didn't look happy."

"You think so?" June said, looking even more radiant. "You really think so?"

"I do. But look, we probably only have a few seconds. Justin's going to notice soon, I bet. So tell me what you think about a, oh, a new crazy idea that I have." He rushed to get his thoughts out. "What if I showed up tonight as Amanda? If I met David face-to-face? Would it be worth the risk, do you think? I thought maybe I could learn for sure whether his feelings have really changed. Or even . . ." and here he drew in a deep breath, "try to change his mind."

June didn't even hesitate. "Oh, I think you should," she said. "How can I help?"

"Something to wear would be nice."

June laughed. "Of course! I'll bring your fancy dress costume to the hotel."

"Would you?" Lionel asked. Then, he looked alarmed. "My hair!"

"Oh, I am so sorry," June said, remorseful again about her slipping scissors. But then she playfully lifted off Lionel's hat and looked at his hair more critically. "You know, I think there might be just enough to hold a little curl. I'll bring hairpins. And fresh flowers in a wreath? I could drop them off at your room."

"You are the best." Lionel grinned just as Justin was turning his head around, searching for them. He tapped David on the shoulder, and they both stopped to wait next to St. Michael's dormitory, a few yards ahead of the playing field. "Could we meet at my room at, say, six o'clock? Will you have time? Zozobra starts at seven?"

"I think I can make it, but it might be close," June said. "I'd better leave now. I'll think of something to tell them," she whispered as they drew up to where the boys stood.

"Thought we'd better stop. I didn't want us to get separated at the grandstand," Justin said.

"Oh, Justin, David," June said. "I was just telling Lionel that I've got a terrible headache. I think Fiesta is catching up with me. And, you know, I can't bear to miss Zozobra so I'm going to have to skip the bullfight and polo. I'm going home to lie down for an hour or so. I'm so sorry." She rubbed her fingers against her temple.

"I'll walk you home," Justin said.

"No, no," June said. "I'm right around the corner. I don't want to spoil anyone's afternoon." She turned to Lionel. "The bullfight is always fun, Lionel. You all go ahead. I'll see you at Zozobra!" and then she hurried away before anyone could protest.

David, Lionel, and Justin stood together for a moment, stunned and stranded. Lionel pressed his fingers to his mustache and pulled out his watch. Justin stretched his neck every few seconds to keep track of June. David's eyes remained on the ground. They each appeared to be thinking of a reason to leave, but when no one offered an excuse, they continued as a group toward the field. Hundreds of people, gathered at the parade's end inside a huge circle of Model Ts, Packards, and Studebakers, were roaming the area, searching for friends and family. An even larger number had packed themselves into the bleachers. David halfheartedly pointed to an empty spot on one of the higher benches when Justin said, "You know, I'm a little worried about June. You go ahead," and took off.

David and Lionel stood awkwardly, but neither spoke. Finally, David started climbing the grandstand, and Lionel followed. Volunteers on the field were herding parade participants out of the ring of automobiles so they could prepare for the bullfight.

"So you'll be taking off for California soon?" David asked after they had settled in their seats. He thought he'd better say something, even though the last person in the world he wanted to be alone with right now was Lionel. He'd barely spoken to him all afternoon and would have preferred to keep it that way. Ironic, considering that being able to talk with Lionel was one of the first things that had attracted him.

"Tomorrow," Lionel said. Was this his chance? He wondered if he should reveal himself right there and then. Get it over with. But it didn't seem right. Not in a crowd. What if David really were in love with June? Now that he knew June didn't feel the same . . . how would he tell David? And if it wasn't June? How could he face David here if he was really in love with someone else, someone who might return that love? No, he'd better stick with his plan and surprise David later. Whatever the truth, he wanted to look like Amanda when he heard it. Besides, there was always the possibility that the sight of her might sway David. Make him think twice, anyway. "I've had a wonderful time. You've all been so kind. But I can't stay forever."

"Couldn't you?" David asked, then, realizing how it might sound, quickly amended, "Obviously you have to be in Hollywood for the movies."

"I'll send a note as soon as I'm settled," Lionel said, "so we can all stay in touch." On the field, several men were dragging a huge papier-mâché bull into the arena, while a matador leaned against the hood of a Model T. Thank god for distractions, thought Lionel. "Oh, look, there's the bull!" Lionel said. "Who's the matador?"

"Señor Armijo," David said.

"His costume is nearly as handsome as mine," Lionel said, thinking back to the baile. "Don't you think?"

David's cheeks flushed with embarrassment. "Very authentic," David said curtly. Taken aback by the sudden change in tone, Lionel decided to shut his mouth and simply watch. At the sound of horns, Matador Armijo walked onto the field, where he flourished his cape, like Lionel had done with the children at the baile. Back then, it had been easy to talk with David. Back then, David had still been in love with Amanda.

In front of the stationary bull, Matador Armijo strutted and flashed his cape. He swung his sword in circles. He struck poses. He performed fancy footwork, gliding to the right of the bull, then to the left. It reminded Lionel of the hoop dance, although its purpose was merriment instead of revelation. Enjoying the sight . . . and remembering to temper his laugh . . . he noticed the inane scene was helping David unbend a little. In a sudden rush of warmth, Lionel vowed never to cause him a moment's pain. No matter what. He loved listening to David's chuckles as the matador performed a perfect backflip over the bull. We could be so happy together, Lionel thought wistfully.

After several minutes of bravado, the matador finally struck the beast with his sword, and the crowd cheered. Lionel wished he could burst into his own real laughter and take David's hand. Instead he concentrated on Señor Armijo, now mounted on a big black mare, which had begun to drag the bull carcass off the field. Suddenly a piece of the bull's tissued pelt tore off and spun in the wind, causing the mare to pitch and kick its back legs into the papier-mâché construction. The crowd gasped at this piece of unexpected drama until Señor Armijo finally managed to gather in his horse while Gus Baumann, the bull's creator, ran down from the stands to assess the damage. His right thumb swung high to show it could be repaired.

"Oh dear," Lionel said, still laughing along with David. What a shame he had to leave just as he and David were beginning to relax. This is what I want, he thought. Feeling comfortable with someone. Happy. Once again he was tempted to tell the truth. But June would be expecting him at La Fonda at six. He'd stick with the plan. "I'm afraid I can't stay for the polo, David. I'm sorry to leave you on your own. But you'll tell me about it at Zozobra?" Lionel had intended to offer a weak excuse about sending a telegram, but it didn't seem to occur to David to ask.

"Of course," David said, and Lionel detected relief. Was he planning to run to his new love the minute Lionel left his side?

"I'll meet you at city hall at seven then?" Lionel asked.

"We'll watch for you," David said. He held out his hand.

On his own in the stands, David felt disturbingly disoriented by the pleasure he had felt as his hand had touched Lionel's. It nearly wiped away his feelings of rejection, which had consumed him ever since their conversation at Indian Fair. The last hour had been pure torture. Nearly . . . there'd been a few moments, when both had been enjoying the sport on the field, when David had begun to feel comfortable again. But remembering that Lionel didn't feel the same . . . oh, if only he could forget about him. He could hardly wait for June's dumb plan to work so she and Justin could finally get together—at least there would be one happy ending—and he could head back to Albuquerque, erase these peculiar couple of days, and get on with his life. The whole idea—his liking men—disturbed him. And why not? Thoughts of Lionel were the sweetest fantasy. But if this were his life? Ahead would be days of hidden impulses and cover stories. And who could he tell? Santa Fe, thanks to the artistic crowd his mother ran with, was more open than other places, but life with another man would never be simple. Ask Hal. And what would his mother say? She expected a daughter-in-law, grandchildren. How would she take the news?

But what else could David do? Lionel thrilled him. And biology was biology, wasn't it? If he was this drawn to Lionel, then that was the truth. If it didn't work out with him, then David would likely be attracted to another man. Unless he managed to talk himself into suppressing these feelings. He didn't know which was worse, realizing he didn't have a chance with Lionel or hoping he did. Maybe he'd been too obtuse, back at Indian Fair, with his hints. Maybe Lionel hadn't even realized what David had been trying to say. He was sure Lionel was interested in guys. Just not David? He'd have only one more chance to explain. Tonight, at Zozobra.

Thinking about how to convince Lionel, David noticed Hal Bynner on his way to a food vendor near the street, stopping to talk with two men, friends from one of the pueblos. The shoulders of all three were shaking—even at this distance, Hal's laugh swung across the field like the whoop of a crane. Hal had probably just shared one of his notorious jokes. He was always the life of the party—David had to admit he'd love to be like that.

He wondered, did he have the nerve to ask Hal for advice?

David inched his way down the grandstand benches, then headed toward Hal with the confused feelings of a would-be compatriot. In the shade of a cottonwood, Hal was now alone, unwrapping a tamale he had ordered from the stand—really just a picnic basket on a bicycle, which this minute was racing away down College Street. Hal took a bite, then raised his hand in a wave as David continued toward him.

"I'm very sorry, I took the last tamale," Hal said. "But not to worry. He's coming back with more—his grandmother's house is right around the corner, apparently. I ordered another dozen to share with friends in the stands."

"Oh, that's all right," David said. "I can wait. I bet they're good."

"Delicious enough to be eaten by gods. Or me. You don't mind . . .?"

"Oh, no," David said. "Please, go ahead."

Hal smiled in thanks and took another bite.

"Mr. Bynner," David said, "I wonder. Would you mind if I ask you something?" He glanced around. They were quite alone at the moment. He drew in a deep breath. "It's kind of sensitive."

Hal, still chewing, nodded in encouragement.

"It's just that, well, that, yesterday I discovered . . . I mean, I felt something yesterday and I just wanted to say that . . ." He leaned forward and spoke quietly into Hal's ear. "I have a question about liking boys."

Hal's eyes grew wide. He took a big swallow.

"Here?" Hal asked. "Perhaps you'd prefer to stop by the house later this week?"

David took a step backward, feeling a fool. "I'm so sorry, Mr. Bynner. I shouldn't have said anything. Never mind. I'll leave." His shoulders slumped as he turned toward the gate.

"No, wait," Hal said, and David stopped. This time, it was Hal who scanned the area for anyone within earshot. "It's obviously important enough for you to ask. You were wondering . . . ?"

"It's just that . . ." Beginning to stutter again, David

decided he'd better plunge ahead. "I met this guy, and I've fallen for him. Hard." He blushed at his word choice. "I've never felt like this. About anyone." He thought for a moment about Amanda. Until he'd met Lionel, that was the closest he'd ever come to love. And it had felt real at the time. But having spent the last two days with Lionel, these feelings were even stronger. "And I'm pretty sure he likes boys. And, well, something like this? It's never happened to me before. So, I guess I don't know how to go about it. I tried talking to him, but he just brushed me off. Like he didn't understand what I was saying."

Hal pulled a handkerchief from his pocket to wipe his fingers, nodding at David to continue.

"I'm not sure what to do now. It's, well, pardon me for saying this, Mr. Bynner, but the way he makes me feel? It's exactly what I was hoping for. I just didn't think it would be a boy. Sorry. Well, you know better than me. It's not the easiest life. Even if he does make me happy. Or, could." David paused. It was never comfortable for him to look anyone in the eye, and it was especially hard now. The shadows from the cottonwood leaves stippled their faces, and David could feel Hal's eyes on him. It reminded him again that one of the first things he had liked about Lionel was how easy it was to be with him.

Hal remained quiet, his expression radiating empathy.

"So, anyway, my question is . . . even though I tried once to tell this boy how I feel, should I try again? I'm going to see him tonight, maybe for the last time. Is there, perhaps, a secret code or something? If I don't say something, I don't think I'll get another chance."

"I have to say, this brings me back," Hal said, touching David's shoulder lightly, then leaning against the trunk of the cottonwood behind him. "The feelings you're having right now."

David nodded, anxious for an answer.

"So let me think. You said, as far as you know, this young man, he feels the same? About boys, I mean."

"As near as I can tell," David said. "I saw him with someone who . . ." and then he stopped. He didn't want to tell Hal about Lionel and Bob Hunt. "I'm pretty sure."

"And why do you think tonight's your last chance? I hate to sound like an old person," Hal said. "But that's usually not the case. There's generally another opportunity. And it might be best to wait."

"He's leaving town," David said.

"I see." Hal folded his arms across his chest. The silver buttons on his purple shirt winked at David. "Because it's best to tread carefully, unless you're sure he's sympathetic." David thought back to La Fonda's dining room, when he and Justin had first mentioned Hal to Lionel. He had seemed pretty skittish then. Was that the real Lionel? Or was it the one who had walked out of the baile with Bob Hunt?

"Though no one knows better than me that, when it comes to love, we have no say in the matter," Hal added, looking toward one of the lower rows in the grandstand. An arm reached up out of the crowd and waved.

"And there's no secret code," Hal said, laughing a little. "Would that there were. But, after a while, you do get a feeling. Word of mouth, at the very least. So, like I said, it might be better to wait and see. But if you're dead set that this is the last time you'll see him—and you have an opportunity for a quiet conversation—I don't think there's harm in trying. But keep it open. You may be right about his inclinations, but maybe even he doesn't know about them yet."

"Believe me, I understand," David said.

"And one more thing, if you don't mind my getting a little philosophical. Your whole life is ahead of you. Today is just one day. There will be plenty more. Plenty of people, too. So, I guess I'd say . . . whatever else you end up doing tonight, just be square with yourself. Accept the liking of those who like you. Like those you like. And to hell with the rest." He laughed. Behind them, the bicycle with its basket of tamales clattered up the street.

When David, still serious, didn't respond, Hal's expression became even more thoughtful.

"And one last thing," Hal said. "I do wonder . . . and I say this with the most open mind I can muster." He pushed himself away from the cottonwood's trunk and stood straight. Three girls from the stands were nearing them to wait for the tamale vendor. "I am quite content. In fact, I prefer being me to anyone else." He grinned. "I say that with a smile, but also sincerely. As you noted, the life is not easy. Though, perhaps, some day . . ." He trailed off, imagining some more enlightened future. Meanwhile, the girls had clustered in a group, a few yards away. Hal lowered his voice even further.

"But there can be much joy. So I would never want to discourage you. And I certainly don't mean to disparage your attraction. But, as I said, after a while you get a sense. So I wonder . . . I wonder if you may be confused about this particular boy? I don't quite see it. For you. If you don't mind my saying. So, let me suggest again, it might be best to wait?"

"Señor!" the vendor called, striking the kickstand on his bike and then pointing to the packaged tamales.

"I'll think about it," David said. What the heck did Hal mean? That he didn't think David could attract a man? Or be attracted to a man? That made him feel even crazier. "I appreciate your time. And the advice. Truly. You've given me a lot to consider." They shook hands.

But not what I wanted, David thought, as he left by the gate. Not the advice he had hoped for.

"Tell him how you feel. You'll be surprised. All will end well."

ELEVEN

Justin's decision to leave David and Lionel had generated a huge physical release. As he shouldered his way against the tide of people entering the grandstands, his limbs seemed to push out in a surge of power. He turned toward the street where June and he were neighbors. If June had gone back to her house, as she said, she ought to be only a block or so ahead. He quickened his pace, trying to catch sight of her, but at Manhattan Street, there was no sign. Cutting through the alley between Santa Fe Avenue and Manhattan Street, a shortcut he'd been taking since the first grade, he slipped into his backyard and decided to climb into the cottonwood that shaded the back half. As a teenager, he'd spent hours in the tree. Now he crouched there, watching for June's approach. A few seconds later, he spotted her at the corner of Webber and Santa Fe. A minute later, she turned at her front walk. He let out a huge breath, unaware that he'd been holding it, and carefully relaxed his position, settling his back comfortably against the limb. She had been telling the truth.

What was the matter with him, anyway? Now that he had seen her safely home, he had to wonder. Did he think she was heading for some secret rendezvous? With whom?

For heaven's sake, both David and Lionel were at St. Michael's, watching the bullfight. What did he think, that there was a third man? It was exhausting, trying to keep track of her love interests. He was still sure that June and Lionel had met before, but had no idea why she would be keeping that secret. Did her parents not approve of him? Had this been arranged so they could see each other secretly? But, if that were the case, why was she here and Lionel at the bullfight?

With David. Remembering June touching David's arm at the parade, Justin thought his heart would come undone. He steadied himself by clutching the tree branch above him. Was it David, after all, that June had finally fallen for? Or was David just June's decoy, a way to keep all eyes away from her and Lionel? At the parade, Lionel had clearly been riveted by the sight of June's arm on David's. Yet when Justin pointed them out, Lionel had simply replied, calm as could be, "Oh, June is so lovely." If he was in love with June, he knew how to hide it.

June and Lionel, June and David. The truth was Justin wasn't happy with June touching anyone's arm. How had he missed how attractive she'd become, that little kid he'd been pals with all these years? He must have been blind. Rushing after this girl, rushing after that. Forbidden fruit? What was the matter with him? All the time, the sweetest, loveliest girl in the world was living right next door. He ought to have his head examined.

Then he recalled talking about June with Lionel and David at Hal's party. Lionel had said something about June being a girl someone could definitely become interested in. And what had Justin answered? "Oh, June. She's a gem. A nice girl. A very nice girl. But like a sister to me."

The memory caused his heart to constrict. He might as well have been throwing them at her.

But now his eyes were open. There was still time. June had a headache and she was resting, just as she'd said. He would start tonight, at Zozobra. If he played his cards right, his current worry over June would sail away with everyone else's cares when they burned that giant marionette, Old Man Gloom.

Intent on imagining ways to win June's heart, he was startled to hear June's front door latch. He looked at his watch and realized he'd been sitting in the tree for over twenty minutes. From his vantage point, he saw her set a large package, wrapped in brown paper and tied with string, onto the swinging bench on the porch. Then, carrying a basket down the front steps, she detoured to the side garden and began cutting flowers. A headache remedy? Justin plastered himself against the tree trunk, hoping to remain invisible. Good Lord, if she saw him, what would he say?

She cradled the full basket, which overflowed with chrysanthemums, cosmos, and a few sunflowers, heading back to the house. She disappeared for several minutes, then returned to the porch, the flowers wrapped in paper like a bouquet. She cushioned the bouquet against her chest, picked up the package by the string, and started up Santa Fe Avenue toward Webber Street.

Justin leaped down from the tree and ran into his own house. He was still in his vaquero costume. Throwing off the serape and bandana, he hurriedly exchanged them for an old gardening jacket and cap that hung by the back door. He called for his father, but there was no answer. He was likely at St. Michael's. The mask Justin had worn at the baile was still lying on the kitchen sideboard, where he'd thrown it. He grabbed it before tearing out the back door and into the alley. Close to Webber Street, he huddled next to a neighbor's tool shed. With any luck, he would soon catch sight of June.

He heard steps. Flattening himself against the shed, Justin observed her walking briskly up Webber to Manhattan in the direction of the Plaza. Justin adjusted the mask over his eyes and nose, then set off behind her. Most of Santa Fe was crowded into the bleachers at St. Michael's, enjoying the game of polo that followed the bullfight, so few others were on the street. Screams of support and groans of disgust thundered from the polo crowd, but June seemed intent only on her errand. She turned down College Street, then took the path through the orchard at De Vargas, adjusting her parcels to carry the bouquet in her left hand. Near the river, she followed the path back onto College Street, crossing the stone bridge and continuing toward the Plaza.

To avoid being seen, Justin was following along the west side of College Street, where he pretended to be looking for an address. He could hear the cathedral's clock chime six. At the same time, a roar of appreciation rose from the crowd. When he next caught sight of June on the bridge, he continued down the street, about a half block behind. Her pace quickened near La Fonda, and she glanced around once before entering. Justin quickly turned to examine a watch in a jeweler's window display.

Then he flew to the front of the hotel, coming into the hotel through the patio. The interior of La Fonda was like a cave after the bright sunlight, and he nearly smacked his head into a doorframe. When his eyes adjusted, he could just make out June talking with Mr. Jimenez, who was parked as usual in the lobby. Then she walked to the elevator and asked for the third floor—Lionel's floor! Justin climbed the stairwell they had used earlier to get to the roof. At the third floor, peering down the hallway, Justin saw June, her eyes alight with excitement, knocking at a door. Then Lionel's arm reached out to lift the parcel from June's grip before pulling her into the room. She was laughing.

It shocked Justin into a statue. He shook his head, hoping to reassemble those last few images into something more comprehensible. June and Lionel? In a hotel room? He should have felt triumph at such vindication of his suspicions, but he only felt ill. Still wearing his mask, he slumped onto the top step, back against the wall. Blood rushing to his head, he wanted to pound on the door and confront them and their secret. He started to his feet. But if he went through with it? There'd be a public scene. And then a scandal. At least he could spare June that. He slumped back onto the step.

What to do? The thought of June and Lionel together in that room maddened him. All that talk at the picnic, June and Amanda's excitement over the New Woman. That's what he thought it had been. Talk. It never occurred to him she would put it into practice. But she could be doing just exactly that, right this minute. She had certainly entered of her own free will. Exuberant, even. But what was in that package . . . some revealing negligee? Justin groaned. And for heaven's sake, Lionel had her bringing flowers? Was that part of being a New Woman? Justin thought again about June's behavior around David. Did David know about Lionel? Would he want to know? He saw again

June's hand resting on David's arm, heard Lionel saying, "Isn't she lovely?"

Justin just couldn't believe it. There had to be some sensible explanation. Perhaps Lionel was ill and had called June to bring him some headache powder. In a large brown bag? Fine, perhaps June brought the headache powder along with an extra blanket for him. She was so generous, always looking out for others. And then she'd thought to bring flowers, to cheer him up. That was it. She'd be out in the hallway in another minute, maybe two. But the door remained closed.

Was it only a few minutes ago that he'd been sitting in the tree, determined to start anew and declare his love? And now—now!—she was lost to him. An ache so sharp pierced his chest that he wondered if his heart really had broken. June, June, June. How could he have let this happen? By god, if he ever had another chance, he'd be the one bringing the flowers! But it was hard to think straight with his brain so full of disagreeable, incomprehensible notions, such as . . . June *was* in love. With someone for whom she felt such passion that she was willing to compromise her reputation. Apparently, she didn't care two figs for Justin. Now he would never get his chance, never have the opportunity to surprise her with kisses or hold her in his arms. She was headed to a life—or ruin!—with Lionel.

He wondered again if he really might be suffering heart failure. He stared at Lionel's door for another five minutes. It remained resolutely shut. Justin finally picked himself up, steadied himself with a grip on the handrail, and stumbled down the steps.

On San Francisco Street, Justin took off his mask, stuffing it into the huge pockets of his father's gardening jacket. He looked around at the nearly empty streets, unable to decide where to go or what to do. Another roar from the direction of St. Michael's decided him. He had better find David, so he could share the misery. David would have to believe him now.

TWELVE

It had been a long time since Amanda had worn a skirt. She liked the way the material flew out with each step. Wouldn't it be wonderful if people could choose between skirts and slacks? But never mind that now. Her right hand, so accustomed to smoothing the mustache, now patted the top of her head, ensuring the wreath of mums and cosmos that June had managed to weave remained in place around her—very short—curls. June had come armed with a slew of bobby pins. She was a miracle worker. Of course, neither the wreath nor the hairstyle would last beyond tonight, but that's all the time she would need.

Amanda had left La Fonda by the side entrance and was heading away from the Plaza and the crowds that swarmed over it. After finishing with Amanda's hair, June had spied her parents in the crowds making their way to Zozobra. Amanda knew that, sooner or later, she would have to face the Sheehans and confess. But right then all she wanted to concentrate on was David. So when June had left La Fonda to find them, Amanda hurried in the other direction, toward the cathedral. Amanda seemed the lone person walking against a stream of revelers headed toward the vacant lot behind city hall, where they would set Zozobra in flames as soon as it got dark. Wanting a moment alone before she came face-to-face with David, Amanda stopped at the bridge.

David! Just his name produced shivers of pleasure. Was it possible that by evening's end, she would know the ecstasy of being in his arms? June had reassured her that she was not now and never had been in love with David. So if it was June that David had fallen for . . . well, Amanda would be there to console him, wouldn't she?

Or was he already marching toward Zozobra, arm in arm with some other love? She shook her head in despair then, remembering the wreath, touched it. Still secure. Thank god. Her outfit, at least, was fabulous: Aunt Gina's ruffled skirt and the dark-green shawl, edged with black fringe and a swirl of blue and lavender flowers, that she had tried on with June . . . was it just last week? She had to laugh. After hours of blending in as a boy, she suddenly enjoyed the novelty of knowing she looked smashing as a girl. If David really was in love with someone else, she would make him say so right to her face. Just inches away, if she could manage it.

She leaned over the bridge, attempting to catch her reflection in the stream. Unlike the rivers back east, there was barely enough water in this one to serve as a mirror. But from what little she could see, the ruffled maroon mums with delicate pink cosmos sweetly framed her face. She gave another supportive pat to her chestnut curls, then turned to contemplate the foothills, where she had first read David's letter. The one where he had known how to say exactly the right thing. She wanted to think up a response that would be just as perfect. She wanted to create a transformative experience as evocative as the hoop dance.

"Amanda!"

David was suddenly by her side, having approached from Canyon Road. After his earlier talk with Hal, he had roamed the streets around St. Michael's, miserably trying to understand himself. Only a few days ago, head over heels in love with Amanda, he would have been dumbfounded if anyone had suggested he might prefer men. Now he felt insulted that Hal intimated he might not have it in him. For himself, David had few doubts. Though Lionel had never displayed any overt romantic feelings, David was sure there was something between them. Those sparks! Lionel must have felt them too. In fact, as certain as he could be about anything in this world, David believed that Lionel had not only felt them, but encouraged them.

By the time he started along Canyon Road, he realized he couldn't live with himself if he let Lionel leave town without seeing him once more. He had to find out for sure if there was a chance, though he thought he knew the answer. With legs made of lead weights, he propelled himself in the direction of the Plaza, so doleful, with eyes on the ground, that he nearly ran into someone on the bridge. Opening his mouth to apologize, he barked out her name instead.

"Amanda!"

At the sound of his voice, Amanda's whole being ripped into life. But the words she had summoned, words intended to knock him off his feet, evaporated into stunned silence. Mutely, they surveyed each other.

His head full of Lionel, his emotions reeling in confusion, David still managed to take in Amanda's beauty. Why hadn't she stayed? he lamented. Three days ago, he would have given his right arm to see this lovely vision in

Santa Fe. Now he felt a dismay so profound it seeped into his bones.

Amanda, amazed to find David at her side, and alone, glowed with happiness, leaning toward him. But even though she could tell that he was practically drinking her in, he also seemed to be constructing an invisible barrier to keep her out. His new love must be powerful, she thought, for him to steel himself against her this way. Disappointment so completely masked her initial delight that she seriously considered fleeing. As usual. This must stop, she thought. Hadn't she come to the Southwest to discover her core self? She was pretty sure she had found her. So she had better make good on her quest and be the person she knew she could be.

"It's good to see you, David," she finally managed. She reached out a hand at the same time that he stuffed his own in his pockets. Her fingers ended up brushing his elbow. She stared at her hands and then, turning toward the water, placed them on the stone railing instead. "I was looking for you. Or, at least, I would have been looking for you. June knows I'm here, and she said I might see you at Zozobra." She turned her head for a quick glimpse at his expression, but he had also turned and, like hers, his eyes were focused on the water. In the stream, the reflection captured the two of them in patches, like a quilt of light.

"Your letter reached me, David. Literally. And emotionally. It made me turn right around and head back to Santa Fe." David went so still, she wasn't sure he was even listening. "You were so courageous to write that letter, David. I know I didn't give you any encouragement at all during those few hours we had together. I was so full of myself." She chanced another look, but he remained frozen

156

in place. She decided to plunge ahead regardless. "But if I had looked or listened, I would have realized that you saw me. Really saw me. And now I want to return the favor. I want to learn and love all that's you." She waited for a response, but he seemed intent only on perusing the stream below as it rustled between rocks, shifting fallen dried leaves.

After a long pause, still concentrating on the ripples below, David began to speak. "I'm so sorry, Amanda. I feel terrible." Amanda's heart sank. "I admire you. I do. Your desire to find yourself, to steer your soul toward a path of meaning. I'm awed by your spirit, Amanda. The words in the letter were the truth. At least, as I knew it then. And I hope we can remain friends."

Now Amanda, who had been listening for encouragement, grew still at his words. Steeling herself for whatever would come next, she turned to face the east. When this was over, she'd walk up to the foothills, skirt be damned. Then the train home. It wouldn't be running away. It was the sensible course now.

"But, since I sent that letter, I feel like I've come face-to-face with my own deepest desires. I guess I've uncovered my own core self." He laughed ruefully. "It wasn't exactly what I expected. But, now that I've found it, I mean to follow it." He turned so that he was looking at her, but she kept her own eyes centered on the ridge in the distance. "I'm so sorry, Amanda. I never expected this. But I've fallen deeply in love with someone else."

"Oh, David," Amanda said softly. A tear glistened in the corner of her eye, and seeing it, David placed his hand on her shoulder. Amanda tried to smile while covering his hand with hers. "I'm happy for you. I guess." She tried to laugh. "It all seems so complicated. You were in love with me, now I'm in love with you." She grimaced. "Someone should make out a schedule for these things. Get us on the right track."

When she heard his shy laugh, she continued. "It's time I confessed something, though, David. It wasn't only the letter that changed my feelings." Now that the time had come to explain, she wasn't sure exactly how to go about it. But she recalled the relief she had felt after unburdening herself to Alfonso. It gave her the motivation to keep going. "I've . . . well . . . I don't know how else to say it. I've been here, David. In Santa Fe. With you, even." When she saw David's puzzled expression, she laughed through her tears. Then she patted her hair. "I was in disguise. As Lionel?"

"Lionel!" David said, looking completely bewildered.

Amanda first set her index finger above her lip. Then she lifted up her elbows and encircled her eyes with her fingers. "Mustache?" she said, her voice lowered. "Glasses?" Then she assumed her normal tone. "I never had any intention of fooling you on purpose. It all began with Justin."

"Justin?" At this, Amanda turned to face David, who was now even more perplexed. She wanted to tell him everything, even though he was lost to her.

"Oh dear, I'd better start from the beginning. You know how crazy June's always been about Justin. And, even though anyone with half a brain could see that they were made for each other, apparently, he had no brain at all. What an idiot that boy can be. Anyway, after the picnic? June and I had cleaned up from our day in the mud." Amanda, seeing David's flustered expression, said, "Honestly, David, I never had so much fun in my life. Quit worrying. Anyway, I asked June to trim my hair, and then we got to talking, and I stupidly spilled the beans about Justin's behavior around Teresa and she was so upset that the scissors slipped and, oops, look at my hair!" She tugged on one of her curls, pulling it out to its full length of two inches. "I mean there is bobbed hair, and then there is no hair, you know?" She laughed.

"So, faced with clipped hair, a decision to masquerade as a boy struck you as the simplest solution?" David asked, not knowing whether to smile or roar in anger.

Amanda laughed. "Well, yes. Though it does seem a bit drastic, when you put it that way. But, think about it. I mean, I guess I could have worn a hat every waking hour. Or joined a convent. But, I really wanted to find out what was going on with Justin. As a favor to June, who's always been so good to me. Even at my most annoying." She shuddered. "But, mostly, I just thought of it as an adventure. To find out what I was made of."

"So you became Lionel?" David asked. Amanda nodded. "Then that means . . . that's how you read the letter!" He looked so relieved—Amanda felt a little hurt because he seemed to have forgotten all about disappointing her in love. "I figured that letter must have sprouted wings to make it to Boston in time to meet you at the other end. Oh, Amanda, this is marvelous!" He held his arms wide and then drew her into them. "My dearest, sweetest Amanda."

For a moment, Amanda was so elated over having David's arms around her that everything suddenly seemed terribly simple. But then she pulled back, and looked at David squarely. "Wait. How can this be marvelous? You just declared yourself madly in love with someone else and miserable about having to tell me so. What are we doing? What are *you* doing?"

"With Lionel," David said. "I was madly in love with Lionel." He laughed out loud. "Amanda, it's been the most confusing week of my life. But I've never felt better."

"Lionel!" Amanda's eyes widened in surprise. "That's who you threw me over for? For me?"

"I'm so sorry to have been unfaithful, dear. But I hope you'll understand."

And then, despite being in the middle of the street, with stragglers still making their way to the lot near city hall, they kissed, and hugged, and kissed again. Pulling apart, David surveyed the top of Amanda's head and, smoothing the wreath back into place, said, "And, oh, by the way, I like your hair."

Lightheartedly, hand in hand, they joined the others heading for Zozobra, happy to be together. And their future? They would find a way, embracing uncertainty. "I feel like I've already let my cares go, don't you?" Amanda asked. "I'm not sure Zozobra's release will be quite as cathartic now. But we ought to attend. Maybe there's a little care we've forgotten. Better make sure we're covered. Besides, I want to tell June."

David let out a laugh so loud it startled Amanda. "And I want to tell Justin." In happy bliss, they exchanged stories about what and how they had been feeling for the past few days. Passing La Fonda, David shook his head over how well Amanda had disguised herself.

"I always thought Justin had some suspicions about my disguise," Amanda said.

"He had suspicions all right," David responded. "But not about your disguise." Just then, he caught sight of Justin, who was standing in front of La Fonda as if waiting for someone. "Justin!" he called out. Justin's mouth fell open when, turning in the direction of David's voice, he caught sight of Amanda.

"Well, I never!" Justin exclaimed. "Amanda, when did you get here? David! You and . . . ?" His questions crowded into one another. "But, David, wait . . ." Justin said as he pulled David aside, leaving Amanda to stand alone on the sidewalk. "Sorry, Amanda. I just need him for a second." He spoke into David's ear. "I've been trying to find you for half an hour! June went home, like she said, and I felt pretty foolish about following her. But . . . I was right after all. Because she left again. She went to La Fonda. She's there now. In Lionel's room," he added miserably.

"Lionel's room!" David said. His face had transformed from anxious interest to amusement, but Justin hadn't noticed.

"The truth is . . ." Justin continued. "Well, I hope you won't think badly of her—but the moment I saw her enter that room, well . . . it's made me insane, to tell you the truth. I don't know how I'll live with it." Justin looked down. "So I went to find you. Because I had seen the way she looked at you. Her hand on your arm. Her smile aimed solely at you." He looked over at Amanda, who was growing impatient. "Well, maybe that doesn't matter to you now. But it made me crazy. June acting like she loved you. And then sneaking off to be with Lionel!" He hung his head. "When I couldn't find you at the polo game, I returned to Lionel's room and I knocked loud enough to be heard on the street. But they never answered. So, either they've left, or . . . worse, if you know what I mean." In the deepening twilight, David recognized Justin's pained expression.

"It's fine, Justin. Really." he said. "You're never going . . ."

"That's fine for you to say, David."

"No really," David said. He turned toward Amanda and held out his hand. "Hey, Lionel. Come meet my friend, Justin."

Amanda, delighted by David's warm smile, walked over and put her arm around his waist. "That Lionel," Amanda said. "Everyone seems to have fallen for him. Don't tell me you think June likes him?" she asked.

Justin's eyes widened. "You mean? You? Lionel? All along?"

"It's a very long story, Justin. Miles long. We'll explain later," David said. "But here's what I'd suggest you do in the meantime. Go find the love of your life . . . just to be clear: that would be June . . . and make sure she knows it! We'll be right behind you."

"Just June? No Lionel?" Justin stammered in his confusion.

"Just June," David said. "Like I said—go!"

Justin headed down the block to city hall, where the crowd had gathered. Arms linked, Amanda and David followed behind. In the vacant lot, the huge open mouth of a twenty-foot puppet leered down at the gathering. With darkness falling, the crowd milled around, excited talk and laughter jamming the air. June was waiting at the edge of the lot, on watch for her friends. When Justin saw her, he hesitated one second, then barreled forward, catching her in his arms. "I've been so worried about you!" he said to her, while she, perplexed but happy, smiled at Amanda and David over his shoulder.

"June!" Amanda called. "Look! I found David!"

Then the four weaved their way through the crowd to where June's parents stood with Jim, Teresa, and Christopher, who had arrived that afternoon—surprising both his astonished mother and an elated Teresa. After hugs all around but before Mrs. Sheehan could say anything to Amanda—eyebrows raised in warning—Amanda spoke first. "I promise to tell you all and I beg for your forgiveness." She kissed June's mother on the cheek. "There's a happy ending, I promise."

By then, with darkness all around, shrouded figures at the base of Zozobra were lighting fires that crackled green and gold. Dignitaries in black robes and hoods stole about the towering figure while the Conquistadores' Band pounded out a funeral march. In time with the dirge, the mayor solemnly proclaimed Zozobra's death sentence, and Isadoro Armijo echoed the verdict in Spanish. Finally, an enormous ring of bonfires were lit, creating a torrent of vivid multicolored flames. Zozobra began to writhe, speaking to the crowd in screams and growls and groans. Even those who knew full well it was only Will Shuster's chicken wire and cloth were drawn under the spell.

Urged on by the crowd, Zozobra reached a fevered pitch, his whole being crying out while he drew in the worries and anxieties of every resident in Santa Fe and the hills beyond until, at last, with a cascade of sparks and the boom of a hundred exploding firecrackers, he ignited the sky. Every person shrieked, thrusting their arms up into the night. Amanda and David fell again into a long warm embrace. Old Man Gloom was dead. The time for celebration was now.

EPILOGUE

Sparks from the fireplace shoot into the chimney. Fall's sweet, warm, fragrant days have temporarily abandoned Santa Fe. A raging storm hurls chilling raindrops against the windowpane, whipping leaves from trees and flinging them into the sky. Hal Bynner relishes the day's dramatics, so different from the city's usual fare. A poem is forming, but there's no need yet to reach for paper and pen. He drops a note he'd been reading from one of the Sheehans' friends, Amanda, into his lap and gazes at the flames' vivid alterations. Her letter, one page long, gushes with apologies for something she says happened at the baile during Fiesta. She was in costume. A matador. She would be happy to clarify, if he would like, but rather than cause any further pain, instead she merely intimates she may have ruined a friendship just then being formed. She hopes she is wrong, begs him to forgive her, and promises never again to meddle. She wishes him the best. She looks forward to his next book of poems.

Hal remembers the baile and some fellow dressed as a matador. He never did get his name. The character had pestered Bob until, good-naturedly, he had agreed to go for a walk to see how he might help. Bob had come back a little drunk, scratching his head over it. He and Hal had shared a good laugh.

The letter slips from Hal's lap onto the floor. With the poker, he sends it into the flames. Then he settles into his chair, draws a smile from his companion, and reaches for Bob's hand.

Acknowledgments

This work of fiction depended on several historical resources—in addition to those devoted to Witter Bynner and Mabel Dodge Luhan—that provided valuable details about Santa Fe in the 1920s, especially *Turn Left at the Sleeping Dog: Scripting the Santa Fe Legend, 1920–1955* by John Pen La Farge (University of New Mexico Press, 2001). The basket dance and hoop dance descriptions were drawn from several sources, including Pablita Velarde's painting *Basket Dance*; "The Basket Dance" by Aurora Lucero-White Lea in *New Mexico* (n.p., 1953); *Dances of the Tewa Pueblo Indians: Expressions of New Life* by Jill D. Sweet (SAR Press, 1985); *Music and Dance of the Tewa Pueblos* by Gertrude Prokosch Kurath with Antonio Garcia (Museum of New Mexico, 1970); and *Formations of Life: Today's Story of the Hoop Dance* by Saginaw Grant and Brian Hammill (Native Spirit Productions, videodisc, 2006). Photographs of 1920s Santa Fe (Palace of the Governors, Photo Archives, Digitized Collections) and contemporary accounts in the *Santa Fe New Mexican* were essential in visualizing that time. Merchant details and street names were found in the Sanborn Fire Insurance Maps (accessed at the New Mexico State Library) and *The Sturges Pocket Map of the City of Santa Fe,*

1926 (accessed at Golden Library, Eastern New Mexico University).

My deepest thanks to my first readers, Suzanne Wittebort and Mary Jane Willis, whose every suggestion made the story better. My heartfelt gratitude also goes to Patricia White, who found time to share ideas both at the start and finish of this endeavor, and to Kay Marcotte for her insights and assistance. Thanks also to my dear family and friends, who always asked about progress, showered me with support, yet knew not to press for details. Finally, I greatly appreciate the time, interest, and encouragement of the manuscript's reviewers, Anne Hillerman and Kevin McIlvoy, and the editorial and design staff at University of New Mexico Press, especially senior acquisitions editor Elise McHugh, senior production editor Marie Landau, and designer Felicia Cedillos. Because of all of you, I have enjoyed every minute of this Santa Fe Fiesta and am happily sending my cares up in flames!

About the Historical Characters

Witter "Hal" Bynner (1881–1968) was a poet, translator, essayist, playwright, and editor. He was author of twenty volumes of poetry. Born in Connecticut and a Harvard graduate, he first visited Santa Fe, New Mexico, in 1922. He lived there for forty-seven years, thirty-four of them with Robert Hunt. Bynner and Mabel Dodge Luhan became acquainted in Santa Fe. Her generosity pleased him at first, but he soon found her possessive nature intolerable. Bynner also had a house in Mexico; he visited there in 1923 with Frieda and D. H. Lawrence.

Further reading: *Who Is Witter Bynner? A Biography* by James Kraft; *The Selected Witter Bynner: Poems, Plays, Translations, Prose, and Letters* edited by James Kraft.

Mabel Dodge Luhan (1879–1962) came to New Mexico in 1917. She and her husband, Maurice Sterne, moved to Taos in January 1918. She arrived with a personal history of presiding over an expatriate community in Italy devoted to life for the sake of art, then as the famous saloniste of Greenwich Village before World War I. Sterne, a sculptor, was her third husband. She divorced him and married Tony Luhan of Taos Pueblo in 1923. Mabel Dodge Luhan was responsible for encouraging many writers and artists to visit or live in the Southwest, among them D. H. Lawrence. Some of these relationships—so promising at first—degenerated because of her need to dominate and control; however, many friends continued to love and cherish her passionate approach to life.

Further reading: *Mabel Dodge Luhan: New Woman, New Worlds* by Lois Palken Rudnick; *Winter in Taos* by Mabel Dodge Luhan.